Look out for The Elephant!

and

Other Stories

by
ENID BLYTON

Illustrated by

Jane Pape-Ettridge

AWARD PUBLICATIONS

For further information on Enid Blyton please contact www.blyton.com

ISBN 0-86163-587-6

First published by Sampson Low (now part of Simon & Schuster
Young Books) as *Enid Blyton's Holiday Book Series*

This edition entitled *Look Out for the Elephant! and Other Stories*
published by permission of The Enid Blyton Company

First published 1993
7th impression 1998

Published by Award Publications Limited,
27 Longford Street, London NW1 3DZ

Printed in Hungary

CONTENTS

Look Out for the Elephant!	5
Jigsaw Jennie	12
Michael's New Belt	19
Little Emily	35
The House in the Fog	51
Interfering Ina	69
A Spell for a Lazy Boy	82
The Surprising Broom	95
Wanted – A Chatterbox	107
A Peep into the Magic Mirror	125
The Very Fierce Carpenter	137
She Wouldn't Believe It	157
Rain in Toytown	165

Look Out for
the Elephant!

"There's an elephant loose!" shouted Jim, rushing into the school playground. "I just heard a man say so. It's escaped from the circus."

"Where is it, where is it?" cried all the children, rushing round Jim.

"It's in the park – and they're afraid it will trample down all the lovely flowers," said Jim.

"Oh, what a shame!" said Sara. She loved flowers, and she couldn't bear to think of the elephant's great feet trampling and breaking them all.

"They've sent for men with sticks," said Jim. "They'll scare that bad elephant properly. I wouldn't mind chasing him myself."

"But elephants are *nice,*" said Sara.

"I rode on one heaps of times at the zoo. They are gentle and kind. They can't help being big and having enormous feet. I think it's horrid to send for men with sticks!"

"All right, then – *you* go and get the elephant out of the park!" said Jim scornfully. "Go on! See if it will come and eat out of your hand and follow you like a dog! I tell you, big sticks are the only thing to frighten an elephant!"

Sara stood listening to Jim. She was just about to tell him that an elephant *had* eaten out of her hand at the zoo when she had given him a bun – and then a grand idea came into her head!

Now when Sara had an idea she always acted on it at once. So she turned and ran over to the baker's. She bought twelve buns out of her pocket money and put them into her school satchel.

You can guess what her idea was now, can't you? Well, well – whoever would think of such a thing? Only Sara!

She ran down the street and made for the park. It wasn't very far away. There was a place in the hedge she could get through. She squeezed through it, and there she was in the park. Where was the elephant?

Well, he wasn't very difficult to see, as you can imagine. There he stood, waving his enormous trunk to and fro, his great feet very near to a big bed of glorious dahlias.

In the distance Sara could hear shouting, and she guessed that men were coming with sticks.

"They'll only scare him and he'll go

galloping over the dahlias," thought Sara. "I'd better hurry."

So she trotted down the path to where the big elephant stood. She went right up to him.

"You're awfully like the elephant who gave me rides at the zoo," she told him, and he looked down at her out of little, twinkling eyes. He flapped his ears and made a little trumpeting noise.

"Are you asking for a bun?" said Sara, and she put her hand in her satchel. "Well, here's one."

The elephant put out his trunk and took the bun. He swung his trunk up

8

to his big mouth – and the bun was gone! He held out his trunk for another.

"Well, you can have all my buns if you come quietly down this path with me," said Sara, "away from these lovely flower-beds. Your feet are so big, you know. Here you are, here's another bun."

She gave him another, and then began to walk down the path to the park gate. The elephant, seeing that she had plenty more buns, followed her closely, trying to put his trunk inside the satchel.

Sara laughed. "Oh, you wait until I give you one! There you are. Now do come along. We'll soon be at the gate!"

Well, well, well! The men with sticks stopped at once when they saw the elephant following little Sara like a dog.

"Look at that!" they said. "That kid has got old Jumbo eating out of her hand! Send his keeper to that park gate – that will be the place to capture

the elephant. He's not scared any more, or angry. Well, would you believe it!"

Jumbo followed Sara all the way to the gate, eating the buns she gave him – and there at the gate was the elephant's keeper waiting for him! Jumbo was very glad indeed to see him. He loved his keeper.

"Thank you, little girl," said the keeper gratefully. "If it hadn't been for you, poor Jumbo would have been sent racing all over the flower-beds in fright, and he might have done a lot of damage. Now – is there any reward you'd like for getting him to come quietly?"

"Well," said Sara, "I suppose – I suppose I couldn't ride on his head, could I, right past our school? The children would hardly believe it if they

10

saw me there!"

"Yes. Old Jumbo will set you on his head and hold you there with his trunk," said the keeper with a laugh. "Hup, Jumbo, hup!"

Jumbo picked up Sara very gently and set her on his big head. Then, holding her there with his trunk, he set off down the road that led past the school, swaying this way and that.

"Look! LOOK! It's Sara up there!" shouted the children. "Hurrah for Sara! Sara, how did you get there? Oh, SARA!"

It was a lovely reward, wasn't it? She deserved it, though, because she really did have a very good idea!

Jigsaw
Jennie

"You ought to be called Jigsaw Jennie," said George scornfully when Jennie began to do yet another jigsaw.

"Well, if I *like* doing jigsaws why shouldn't I do them?" said Jennie. "You like collecting stamps and Robert likes making things with his Meccano. I don't laugh at you for doing those things whenever you can."

"But you always take up all the table with your silly jigsaws," said Robert. "You go on and on. I can't think what you can see in them."

"And I can't see what George sees in his silly stamps, or you see in your endless Meccano," said Jennie, beginning to be cross. "Can't you see that some people like doing one thing and some another? I'm good at doing something else. I don't see why we can't all be happy in our own way."

"Well, collecting stamps teaches you geography, so it's some use. And making things with Meccano teaches you to be clever with your hands," said Robert. "Doing jigsaws simply doesn't teach you anything."

"I'll do them just for pleasure, then," said Jennie, emptying out a box of coloured jigsaw pieces. "And you never know – you might be glad some day that I'm so clever at fitting jigsaws together!"

"We shan't, Jigsaw Jennie!" said George. "And remember this: when our birthday comes next week *don't* give us jigsaws. We don't like them."

13

"I'm not going to," said Jennie. "I've got your presents already!"

George's birthday and Robert's came very near together – only two days between – so they always shared it and made one big day of it between them. Jennie didn't give them jigsaws, of course. She gave George a new stamp-album and Robert a book showing him all kinds of different things he could build.

They were both very pleased. "We've been lucky," they said. "We've had ships, trains, books – and a five pound note between us!"

"Two pounds fifty each," said George. "Lovely! We're rich!"

"Put the money in your money-box," said their mother. But they forgot and left it on the window-sill. The wind came and blew it away. It blew it inside the room and over to the toy cupboard. It blew it right inside to the very, very back.

So, of course, when the two boys looked for the money, it was gone. They couldn't find it anywhere. They didn't think of looking at the back of the toy cupboard. They were very sad, but it couldn't be helped. The five pound note was gone.

Now a little mouse ran in and out of the toy cupboard each night. It came the night the paper money had blown to the back of the toy cupboard. It was very pleased to find it there, because it meant to make a paper nest. This paper would do nicely! It could bite it up into little pieces and make a cosy little nest in the little toy motor-car.

So it chewed up the note into about seventy pieces and made a nest of it. But before any babies came into the

nest the children's mother turned out the toy cupboard – and she found the mouse's nest in the toy motor-car. She called to the children:

"Jennie! George! Robert! Do come and see. A little mouse has made a nest in your toy motor-car."

They came to look. George gave a cry! "Mother! Look at what the nest is made of – our five pound note all bitten into tiny pieces!"

"It's wasted," said Robert. "We can't spend it now. Oh, what a pity!"

Jennie emptied the tiny bits carefully on to a little tray. She looked at them.

"It's rather like a little paper jigsaw," she said. "If only I could fit all the little bits together properly, and put some sticky paper behind, the five pound note would be whole again and you might be allowed to spend it!"

"Oh, Jennie – *could* you do it?" cried George and Robert. "Begin now, quickly."

So Jennie's deft fingers sorted out

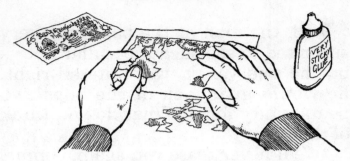

the tiny paper bits. She borrowed a new five pound note from mother to see how it looked, and then she began to do a peculiar jigsaw! A bit here and a bit there. That bit fits there surely, and that one should go there. Here's a straight bit, and here's another!

"It's coming, it's coming!" cried George. And so it was. It took Jennie nearly the whole day to fit the many little bits together and to stick them carefully at the back so that the note showed up whole.

"You're very patient and deft, and very clever, Jigsaw Jennie!" said Mother admiringly. "But I don't think anyone would take the note. We'd better go and ask the man at the bank what he thinks."

Well, the man at the bank was very surprised to see such a peculiar note – but he said yes, it was quite all right, he would give each of the boys two pounds fifty for it! What do you think of that?

"We'll never tease you again, Jennie, never," said George. "You're the cleverest sister in the world. Come and spend our money with us."

They spent it all – and part of it was spent on...well, I'll give you a guess! Yes, you're right – it was spent on a new jigsaw for Jennie. She's going to do it tonight, and you may be sure she will get every single piece into its right place before she goes to bed. Clever Jigsaw Jennie!

Michael's New Belt

Michael was very proud of his new leather belt. It had little brass studs on it half-way round and a rather grand buckle.

"See my belt?" he said to the other boys. "My uncle gave me that. He brought it back from Canada with him. I guess this is the kind of belt that cowboys wear on a ranch over there."

The other boys thought it was fine. They fingered it and patted the brass studs. "Wish I had one like that," said William, the head of the class. Michael was very proud to hear him say that.

Michael was very careful of his new belt. He didn't wear it every day. He kept it for Sundays, or for the days he went to see his granny or his aunts. Then he would buckle the new belt

round his jeans, with the brass studs and buckle shining brightly, and set off proudly.

One day he went to see his granny. He stayed to dinner with her and then set off to walk home. He had on his new belt, of course, and Granny had admired it for the twentieth time.

"I suppose you wouldn't lend it to me to wear when I go to London next week," she said solemnly.

Michael laughed. "Oh, Granny – you

wouldn't want to wear a belt like mine, you know you wouldn't – but I would lend it to you if you really wanted it. I wouldn't lend it to any boy or girl though! It's much too precious!"

He went off home with two little ginger cakes Granny had baked for his tea. And on the way home he heard someone shouting so loudly that he stopped in surprise. Who was shouting? Michael was in the fields and he couldn't see anyone about at all. The shouting went on and on. "Help! Help me! Can't you see me? I'm up here. *Up here!* Up the tree!"

Then Michael looked up, and there, a good way up a tall tree on the other side of the hedge, he saw a boy. The tree was bare, and Michael could see him easily. He stared in surprise.

"I say! Help me, won't you?" yelled the boy.

"Why? What's the matter? Can't you climb down?" yelled back Michael, going nearer the tree.

"No. I've got stuck somehow. And

now I'm frightened," said the boy, sounding almost as if he were going to cry.

"Why did you climb so high?" called Michael.

"There's a bull in this field and he ran at me," shouted back the boy. "I just had time to shin up this tree, and I can tell you I climbed faster than I've ever climbed in my life! Now I'm stuck – and I'm awfully afraid of falling. I feel giddy."

"I'll come up and help you down," said Michael. He kept a look-out for the bull, which didn't seem to be anywhere around, and then began to climb up the tree. He soon reached the boy.

"Look – can't you put your foot down to this branch?" he said to the boy. "What's your name? I don't seem

22

to have seen you before."

"I'm Robert Trent," said the boy. "No – I can't put my foot down to the branch. I tell you, I'm scared. I think I'm going to be sick."

Michael looked at him. He did look rather green.

"You're not *really* afraid of falling, are you?" he said anxiously. "Here – hold on to me until you feel a bit better." The boy wouldn't even hold on to Michael. He wouldn't let go his hold of the branch he was on.

"Isn't there a ladder I can get down by?" he said desperately. "Surely there's one at the farm. I know I shall fall soon."

"I'll go and run to the farm for

23

help," said Michael, beginning to climb down again. But the boy cried out at once: "No! Don't leave me! I shall fall down the tree if you do, I know I shall. Stay with me."

"But that's silly," said Michael, sensibly. "How can I possibly go and get help if you won't let me leave you?"

"I don't know," said the boy, looking greener than ever. "I do feel awful. I daren't even open my eyes now, because I know I shall feel giddy if I do."

Michael looked down the tree. It was a long, long way to fall. He began to feel frightened for the boy. Suppose he did fall? He might be killed – or at least break a leg or an arm.

The boy spoke again, his eyes still shut. "Have you got a rope, by any chance? So that you could tie me to this branch? If you could do that I'd feel safer and I'd let you go and fetch help."

"No, I haven't got a rope," said Michael. And then a thought struck him. He hadn't a rope – but he had got a fine, strong leather belt!

He looked down at his belt. He didn't want to lend it to anyone, not even to Robert. It would probably be rubbed against the tree – some of the brass studs might come out. No, he couldn't think of lending it to this foolish boy.

But Michael was a kindly boy, and he didn't go on thinking like this for long. He suddenly unbuckled his belt and slipped it off his jeans.

"I'll buckle you to the branch with

25

my belt," he said. "That will keep you safe. It's very good, strong leather."

But the belt wasn't long enough to buckle the boy to a branch. So Michael did the next best thing – he buckled the belt loosely to a near-by bough, and told Robert to slip his arm through it. Then he tightened the belt over the boy's arm. "There!" he said.

"Now even if you do feel yourself falling my belt will hold you up. You needn't be afraid any more."

"Oh, that's a wonderful idea," said the boy, gratefully. "I feel better already. Thanks very much."

"I'll go down now and get a ladder or something," said Michael, and he shinned quickly down the tree, glad that he had a better head than Robert for climbing! He ran off towards the farm.

It was a long time before he could find anyone to help him. The farmer and his wife were at market. The men were at work in different places. At last Michael found one who listened to his tale.

"What – a boy up a tree and can't get down!" said the man. "What sort of a boy is that? He's not worth bothering with!"

"But I know he'll fall if I don't get help," said Michael. "Where's a ladder? Can I borrow one?"

"No! A youngster like you can't

carry a great heavy ladder to put half-
way up a tree," said the man. "Wait
until I've finished this job and I'll come
myself."

So Michael had to wait impatiently
until the man finished his work. Then,
not hurrying himself at all, he went
with Michael to the tree in the field
where the bull was. But Robert wasn't
there! He had gone!

"This is the tree," said Michael. "But
the boy's gone! How odd!"

"Look here," said the man, "did you
make this all up, just to play a trick?
Because if you did, I'll..."

"No – I really didn't," said Michael

hurriedly. "Please believe me, I even lent the boy my best leather belt to hang on to, and tied up my jeans with a bit of string – look."

"Well – you won't see your leather belt any more, that's certain," said the man, and went off. Michael stood there alone feeling very upset. Was the man right? Had he really lost his belt for good?

He saw a man in the field, leading the bull with a stick which he had fastened to a ring at the end of the bull's nose. He called to him.

"I say! Did you see a boy up a tree here frightened of falling?"

"Yes. I saw him when I came to get the bull," shouted back the man. "Silly youngster, climbing so high he's scared of falling. I got him down all right."

"Where did he go?" asked Michael. "Did he say anything about a leather belt I lent him?"

"No, he didn't," said the man. "He fastened one round his waist – a beauty it was – and off he went."

"Oh," said Michael. He was upset and disappointed. He had helped the boy – and all the return he got was to lose his belt, and not have a single word of thanks!

He went home and told his mother all about it. "If I meet that boy again I'll fight him!" he said. "He might at least have waited under the tree until I came back, and given me my belt. My beautiful belt! Mother, I'll never lend anyone my belt again – I won't lend anyone *any*thing again. I won't even help people in trouble."

"Now, that's not like you, Michael," said his mother. "You mustn't think

bad of people until you are certain they have done something wrong or unkind. And how foolish to change yourself from a kind, generous boy into an unkind, selfish one just because somebody has behaved badly to you!"

"Oh, well – I expect you're right as usual, Mother," said Michael. "I'll be sensible. But you don't know how upset I am about my belt."

Now, a week after that, Michael went shopping in the next town with his mother. As he was walking down the road, a car suddenly stopped just

31

by him and a head popped out. A voice called excitedly:

"I say, I say! Aren't you the boy who lent me your lovely belt up that tree?" And there was Robert looking out of the car window! Michael nodded, looking rather surly. The boy got out of the car and ran to him.

"A man got me down from the tree after you'd gone. I put on your belt to keep it safe, and then I went off to look for you – but I lost my way and never found you. And ever since I've worried and worried as I was afraid you'd think I'd gone off with it and never meant to give it back!"

Michael didn't know *what* to say!

His mother came to the rescue. "Michael is always lending things to others, and he always gets them back."

A man looked out of the car. "Is this the boy who helped Robert?" he said. "We've been making enquiries about him all over the place. Thank you, sonny, for doing your best for him. He's an idiot to climb trees – he always feels giddy."

"Here's your belt," said Robert, taking a parcel out of the car. "I've carried it about with me ever since last week, hoping I'd see you somewhere. Dad, can we take him to the circus with us? Can he come now?"

"Well – we must ask his mother," said Robert's father. You can guess

33

what Michael's mother said.

"Of course he can come," she said. "Do you mean now, this very minute? Oh, what a surprise for you, Michael!"

It certainly was. In a flash he was in the car, sitting beside Robert, speeding off to the circus. What a wonderful time he had!

And now, of course, Robert and Michael are quite inseparable – in fact, Michael's mother says she never sees one without the other! And will you believe it, Michael lends his belt to Robert whenever he asks him to!

Little Emily

Once upon a time, when your mothers were as small as you, there lived a little girl called Emily.

She was a funny little girl. She never cried, she never grumbled, she never complained about anything. Well, that sounds as if she was very good, doesn't it? Yet nobody liked her!

"Emily's strange," said John, who lived next door. "She never feels sorry for anyone! When I fell over the garden wall the other day, and made my head bleed, Emily just stood and stared at me. It was Jane who rushed up and helped me."

"And you know that poor blind man who stands at the corner of the main road, don't you?" said Katie. "Well, we've given him some money at times – but Emily told me she never had. And when I said 'But aren't you sorry he's blind? Don't you want to help him?' she said No, she didn't. She *is* strange."

"The other day I went to tea with her," said Lennie. "Her mother had a dreadful headache, so I thought we would play a game that didn't make much noise. But Emily shouted and laughed as loudly as anything. And she's got such a nice, kind mother! I think there's something the matter with Emily."

"It's what I said," said John. "She's never sorry for anyone. She's not warm-hearted. She's pretty and clever and neat, and good at games – but you just can't like her!"

Now one day Emily's grandmother came to see her. The poor old lady had fallen down the stairs the day before and hurt her knee, so she could only just hobble along with a stick. But did Emily rush to get her a chair, or put

her footstool for her bad leg to rest on?
Did she kiss her kind old granny and
say she was sorry about her leg?

No, she didn't. She let her mother
get the chair and the footstool. Her
granny looked at her then spoke to her
mother.

"There's something wrong with
Emily. She's never sorry for anyone, so
she's never kind. I think there must be
something wrong with her heart. She's
cold-hearted, and that's a most terrible
thing to be, because she will never
know what it is to be really happy! You
must have a warm heart to be happy."

Emily thought her granny was silly. "I am happy," she said. "And why should I be sorry for people? I am never sorry for myself."

"You have no need to be," said her granny, impatiently. "You are pretty and clever; you have nice clothes and good food to eat. You have a kind father and mother, and plenty of toys. You have no cause to be sorry for yourself. But because you are such a lucky little girl you should be grateful, and try to feel sorry for those who are not so well off, and who may be very ill or unhappy."

"You are always preaching, Granny," said Emily, rather crossly.

Her mother was worried to hear what Granny said and she made up her mind to take Emily to the doctor. So the next day she set off with Emily. The little girl didn't want to go, and she hung behind all the way. But at last they were there and the wise old doctor was looking at the little girl.

He listened to her heart. He felt all

round it. He tapped it. He stroked the skin over it. Then he shook his head.

"It seems all right," he said, "and yet there certainly is something wrong with it. Bring her again soon and I will try and find out what is the matter. Most extraordinary!"

Emily's mother was upset and frightened to hear what the doctor said. As they went through the woods on their way home, she cried and tears ran down her cheeks. Emily saw them, but she didn't bother to comfort her mother.

Soon they met a small bent old woman who lived all by herself in the wood. Everyone thought she must be more than a hundred years old. She

stopped when she saw Emily's mother crying, and asked her what was the matter.

"There's something wrong with my little Emily's heart," said the little girl's mother, "but the doctor doesn't know what it is."

"Well, maybe *I* can find out!" said the little woman. "There's many a spell I know to put hearts right. I'll have a look at Emily's."

"You can't! It's inside me," said Emily. But the old woman only laughed and clapped Emily so hard on the back that her heart flew out of her body, and landed on the grass beside the old woman. It was the strangest thing you ever saw! The old lady bent down and picked up the heart. She

40

shook her head solemnly, and showed it to Emily's surprised mother.

"Look there! Her heart is of stone! Feel it – it's hard and cold. Do you wonder the child can't feel sorry for anyone, and can't do a kindness? Who could, with a cold, hard heart like that! It's the worst heart I have ever seen in my life, and I've looked into a good many. Here you are – take it back, little girl. You'll never be happy until you melt that stony heart of yours."

"But how can she?" asked the mother, frightened and sad.

"Only one way," said the old woman, hobbling off. "Only one way. Be kind, even if you don't feel like it. There's nothing like kindness to melt a heart of stone!"

"Oh, Emily, you must try and do what the old woman says," said her mother. "I do want people to love you, as they love other children. Please will you try to be kind, and see if your heart gets better?"

"Well, I'll try," said Emily, thinking the whole thing was a fuss and a bother. "I really will try. I didn't very much like the look of my heart, I must say. You know, Mother, it has felt very heavy lately; and, of course, if it's made of stone that's the reason!"

Well, you have no idea how hard it is to be kind if you don't feel as if you want to be! Poor Emily – it was difficult for her to say nice things to people, and to try and comfort them when things went wrong. But because she didn't want her heart to feel heavier and heavier she tried.

"When children fall down I must pick them up," she planned. "When they get into trouble over their lessons I must help them. When Mother has a headache I must be quiet. It's easy enough for the other children to do these things, because they *want* to do them – but I don't. Still, I will."

So she did. She had plenty of chances for kindness that week. Mandy, who lived opposite, broke her leg and Emily went across to see her. She took her one of her own dolls, and she read to Mandy for half an hour from a book. She didn't want to one bit, of course. It bored her very much.

At the end of her visit, when she rose to go, Mandy pulled her down to the couch and kissed her. "I never knew you could be so sweet and kind,

Emily!" she said. "I *love* the doll – and you do read so nicely. Please come again!"

Emily suddenly felt a curious pain in her heart, and she put her hand there. She felt pleased with Mandy's words, but she wished her heart wouldn't hurt her so much. It would be too bad if it began to pain her just as she was trying hard to cure it.

The next day she went to see her granny, and she rode in the bus. It was very full, and Emily could only just find herself a seat. As she sat down she noticed an old man getting on the bus. There was no room for him at all. He would have to stand. Emily would have let him stand in the ordinary way, but

now she was trying to remember to be kind. So up she got at once.

"Please have my seat," she said; and the old fellow sat down.

"Now there's a kind little girl for you!" he said in such a loud voice that everyone heard. They stared at Emily, and gave her warm smiles. She felt that funny pain round her heart again, and pressed it hard. Oh dear, it really did hurt!

She went into her granny's house. "How is your poor leg, Granny?" she said. "Don't get up to get tea. I will get it for you, and I'll make you some toast, too."

Emily had planned all this on the bus. Her granny was most astonished. She sat and watched the little girl getting tea.

"Well, you always were a pretty child, Emily," she said at last, "but now you've a bit of kindness in your eyes, you look a real darling. It's a pleasure to have you with me!"

Emily's heart hurt her again, but

she didn't say a word. No – she had always boasted that she never felt sorry for herself, so she wouldn't complain!

A week or two went by. Emily did every little kindness she could. She gave the old blind man tenpence instead of buying a new chair for her dolls' house. She took Mrs Brown's baby out in the pram for her each day, because Mrs Brown was so busy with the spring-cleaning. She brought in a poor half-starved little cat, and asked her mother if she could feed it and keep it for her own. It was the first time she had ever wanted a pet!

She began to look happy, though her heart gave her a lot of pain. She smiled dozens of times in an hour. She

laughed more than she had ever done. Her eyes were bright and shone with a kindness that no one had ever seen there before.

"Emily, I can't help feeling proud of you," said her mother. "You really do try very hard indeed to be kind. Do you still find it very difficult?"

Emily thought hard, and a surprised look came into her eyes. "No," she said. "It isn't hard at all now. I don't have to *try* to be kind, Mother. I want to be. I can't help being. I don't have to think to myself, 'Look, Katie has fallen down. It's your duty to go and help her.' I just rush to her without thinking, because I can't bear to see

47

her crying."

"I'm so glad," said her mother. "Your heart must be quite better now."

"Oh, Mother – it isn't," said poor Emily, pressing her hand on to it. "It's much worse. It gives me such a lot of pain. Sometimes I can't bear it."

"Poor child!" said her mother, in alarm. "We'll go at once to that old woman who lives in the wood. Maybe she can do something. We'll go now."

So they went, and came to the old dame's little hidden-away cottage. She was in, and very pleased to see them.

"Emily really has been trying to be kind," explained the little girl's mother. "But I'm afraid her heart is

worse. It hurts her very much."

"Let's feel it," said the old woman, and she put her hand inside Emily's dress. She felt round about where her heart was. Then she laughed and laughed.

"There's nothing wrong!" she said. "Nothing at all! It's a different heart entirely! It's warm and soft – you feel it yourself, madam! Nothing like the hard, cold heart of stone she had before. It's a lovely heart to have. She should be proud of it now, for a warm heart like that will bring her great happiness. Look at her face – it's sweet and kind now."

"But why does her heart hurt her?" asked the little girl's mother.

"It won't any more," said the old dame. "You see, it's as I said – kindness melted that heart of stone – and the melting was painful. But now it's quite all right. She needn't worry any more!"

Emily was very happy to hear that. She went off with her mother, skipping along. Now she is grown-up and I know perfectly well that her heart is as warm and kind as anyone else's. You should see how the children love her! She told me this story to tell to you, and she says: "Always have a warm heart, and you'll be as happy as the day is long!"

The House in the Fog

There was once a boy who didn't believe in fairies, or pixies, or giants, or dragons, or magic, or anything like that at all.

"But at least you know there were dragons," said Mary. "St George killed one. It's even in our history books at school, where it tells us why we have St George's cross on our flag."

"Believe what you like," said William, "I just don't think there ever were such things."

Now one day William had to go to a Cub Meeting. He was a very good Cub indeed, and meant to be an even better Scout later on. He had his tea at home then looked at the clock. "I must go, Mother," he said. "I've got to be

51

at the meeting at six."

His mother peered out of the window. It was a dark evening – and, dear me, how foggy it seemed, too! "I wonder if you ought to go, William," she said. "It's getting foggy."

"Oh, Mother – what does that matter?" said William, putting on his Cub jersey. "I know my way blindfold! I can't *possibly* miss my way home."

Well, William was certainly a very sensible boy, so his mother let him go. He got to the meeting in good time – William was always punctual – and he had a very nice evening. Then it was time to go home.

The Cub-master looked out of the

door. "My word," he said, "the fog is very thick. I hope you will find your way home all right."

"Well, we all go the same way, except William," said John. "So we can keep together. What about William, though?"

"Pooh!" said William. "Do you suppose I'd lose my way in a fog! A Cub knows his way about even if he can't see a thing!"

And off he went out into the fog alone. Didn't he know his way perfectly well? Hadn't he walked the same road dozens of times? What did it matter if the fog was thick? He could *easily* find his way home.

But after he turned two corners he suddenly stopped. His torch hardly showed a beam at all in the thick fog. Was he in the right road? He must be! He couldn't possibly have taken the wrong turning.

He flashed his torch on the name of the road, printed on a wall nearby. Ah, yes – he was all right – it was Ash Tree Avenue. Thank goodness! He hadn't gone the wrong way after all.

"I've only to go down to the end of the road, turn sharply to the left, cross over, and then keep straight on until I get to my own house," said William to himself. So off he went again, his steps tap-tapping in the fog which now swirled thickly about him.

He went on and on. Wherever was the end of Ash Tree Avenue? Surely it wasn't as long as this! On and on and on. William stopped, puzzled. He ought to have come to the end of it by now, and have turned left.

He turned and went back. "I'll start at the top again, where the name of

the road is," he thought. His steps tap-tapped again as he went. On and on and on he walked.

He didn't come to the beginning of the road, where he had seen the name. Where was it? He had kept on the very same pavement and he hadn't crossed over at all. It *must* still be Ash Tree Avenue. But why didn't it end? He stopped again. He turned and went *down* the road this time. Surely he would come to the turning! On he went, but there really was no turning! What had happened?

"I'm not in a dream, I know that," said William. "I've just come from the Cub Meeting, and I'm walking home in rather thick fog. And I'm on the right way. I'm not lost. I just can't seem to find the end of this road."

It was no use. He couldn't find it. No matter if he went up or down, there seemed no end and no beginning.

"This is absolutely silly," said William at last. "There's no sense in it. I shall go into one of those houses and ask my way."

He flashed the torch on the gate of the nearest house. He saw the name there, MUNTI HOUSE. He went up the little path and came to the front door. It had a peculiar knocker in the shape of a man's head. The head had pointed ears and a wide grin. William knocked on the door with it.

The door opened, and a dim light shone out from the hall. "Please," began William, "could you tell me –"

Then he stopped. Nobody was there. There was just the open door and the dark hall and nothing else. How peculiar! William peered inside.

A curious whistling noise came from the hall, like the wind makes in the chimney. "Well," said William, "if someone is whistling, someone is at home. I'll go in."

So in he went and the door shut softly behind him. He walked up the hall and came to a room without a door. Someone was whistling there. The whistling stopped. "Come in, come in," said a high little voice. "What do you want, William?"

William jumped. How did anyone in that house know his name? He looked round the room in surprise. A plump little man with pointed ears and remarkably green eyes was sitting in a rocking-chair by an enormous fire. Rockity-rock, he went, rockity-rock.

He looked at William and grinned.

"Why," said William, "you are exactly like the knocker on your door!"

"I know," said the little man. "Why shouldn't I be? Your name's William, isn't it? I'm Mr Munti, of Munti House."

"How do you know my name's William?" asked William.

"Well, I just took one look at you and I knew your name must be William," said Mr Munti, rocking furiously. "That's easy."

It didn't seem easy to William. He stared at Mr Munti, who stared back. "I came to ask if you could . . ." began William, but he was interrupted by a large black and white cat with eyes as green as Mr Munti's.

"MEEEE-ow," said the cat, walking into the room and patting Mr Munti on the knee. "MEEEE-ow!"

"Hungry, are you?" said Mr Munti. "Pour, jug, pour!"

There was a pint milk-jug on the table and, on the floor below, a large

saucer. The jug solemnly tipped itself
and poured milk into the saucer below.

"Good, jug, good," said Mr Munti,
rocking away hard. "You didn't spill a
drop that time. You're getting better."

William stared in surprise. What a
peculiar jug! He looked at Mr Munti. "I
say," he said, "are you a conjuror?"

"No," said Mr Munti. "Are you?"

"No," said William. "I'm a little boy."

"Don't believe in them," said Mr
Munti, and he gave a sudden high

chuckle like a blackbird. "I never did believe in little boys."

William was astonished. "But you *must* believe in them," he said. "I've just been to a Cub Meeting. I'm a Cub, and I . . ."

"There you are!" said Mr Munti grinning. "You're a Cub. You're not a little boy. What sort of Cub are you? I believe you're a fox-cub. You've got such a nice bushy tail."

William felt something swishing behind him and looked around. To his enormous astonishment he saw that a fine bushy tail hung down behind him. He turned around to see it properly – and the tail turned with him. He felt it – good gracious, it seemed to be growing on him, right through his trousers!

"MEEEE-ow," said the cat again and patted the little man on the knee.

"What! Still hungry?" said Mr Munti. "I never knew such a cat! There's a kipper in the cupboard for you."

The cat went to the cupboard door, stood on his hind legs and opened it. He sniffed inside the cupboard, put in his paw and pulled out a kipper. It landed on the floor.

"Shut the door, Greeny, shut it," ordered Mr Munti. The cat blinked at him with deep green eyes and carefully shut the cupboard door. Then he began to eat his kipper.

William stared, open-mouthed, forgetting his tail for the moment. What a clever cat!

"Well?" said Mr Munti, rocking away hard. "Did you say you were a fox-cub? Or perhaps you are a bear-cub? I see you have nice hairy paws."

William looked at his hands in horror. Whatever was the matter with him? He had big hairy paws now, instead of hands. He hid them in his pockets at once, full of dismay. What *was* happening? What was this little man with the bright green eyes?

"No – on the whole, I think you

must be a lion-cub," said Mr Munti, peering at him. "I never in my life have seen such wonderful whiskers. Magnificent. Aren't they, Greeny? Even better than yours."

"MEEEE-ow," said Greeny, and began washing himself very thoroughly.

William felt his face in alarm. Goodness gracious, there were long strong whiskers growing from his cheeks – how very peculiar he must look! His paw brushed against his face, a furry, soft paddy-paw, just like a bear's.

"Please, sir," said William, beginning to feel scared, "I want to go home. I'm not a lion-cub, or a bear-cub, or a fox-cub – I'm a little boy Cub, a sort of Scout."

"I told you, I don't believe in little boys," said Mr Munti. "So I don't believe in your home either. I don't believe you want to go there because there isn't one, and I don't believe in *you*. Do you believe in me?"

"Well – what are you?" asked William, desperately.

"My mother was a pixie and my father was a brownie," said Mr Munti, rocking away.

"Then I don't believe in you," said poor William. "I don't believe in fairies, or pixies, or brownies, or dragons, or giants, or . . ."

"And I don't believe in little boys, so we're quits," said Mr Munti, with a wide grin.

"Ding-dong," said the clock loudly, and danced all the way down to the end of the mantelpiece and back again.

"Will you stop that?" said Mr Munti fiercely to the clock. "How often must I tell you that well-behaved clocks don't caper about like that?"

William began to feel bewildered. His tail waved about behind him. He could feel it quite well. His hairy paws were deep in his pockets. He could feel the whiskers on his cheeks. WHAT was happening? He didn't believe in any of it, but it was happening all right

– and happening to him.

"I'm going out of this peculiar house," said William suddenly, and he turned to go.

"You might say goodbye," said Mr Munti, rocking tremendously hard and almost tipping over.

"Goodbye, Mr Munti," said William.

"MEEEE-ow," said the cat, and came with him to the front door. The cat stood up and opened the door politely. William went out into the darkness and the fog. The door shut. He shone his torch on the knocker head, and then on the name of the

house on the front gate – MUNTI HOUSE. Who was Mr Munti really? Was he, *could* he be a conjurer? Conjurers did do peculiar things. But that cat, too – and the jug – and the clock!

"I shall certainly come back tomorrow and see Mr Munti again, in the daylight," said William to himself. He went down the road, hoping that he would find the end of it this time. And, to his great delight, he did. The fog began to clear a little, and he could see his way.

"Turn to the left – then over the crossing – and straight home!" said William, in delight. "Oh dear – what in the world will Mother say when I arrive home with a tail and furry paws and whiskers?"

She didn't say anything – because when William thankfully walked in his tail had gone, his hands were his own again, and there were no whiskers left. And what was more, his mother wouldn't believe a word of his tale!

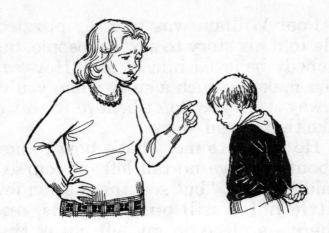

"Fancy you making up such a silly story!" she said. "You're very late, William – and you needn't tell me a lot of fairy-tales like that. Just tell the truth."

Now, the next day, as you can imagine, William went off to Ash Tree Avenue to look for Munti House, and the strange knocker on the door, and Mr Munti himself. And will you believe it, though he looked at every single house in the avenue at least three times, not one was called Munti House, and not one had a knocker in the shape of a grinning head.

Poor William was terribly puzzled. He told his story to several people, but nobody believed him at all. "How *can* you make up such a story when you've always said you don't believe in things like that?" said Mary.

He told it to me. That's how I know about it. "I've no tail left, of course," said William, "but see, there are a few little hairs still on my hands, and there's a place on my left cheek that feels a bit like a whisker growing. Do, do tell me what you think about it, please?"

Well, I don't know what to think! What do you think about it all?

Interfering Ina

I wonder if you ever knew Interfering Ina? She was a little girl about eight years old, quite pretty, quite clever – but, oh dear, how she did interfere with all the other children!

If she saw two or three of them playing a game together she would go and poke her nose into the game and say, "Oh, you are not playing that quite right! Look, you should play it *this* way!"

And then she would make the children play quite a different way, a way they didn't want to play at all!

"Don't interfere!" they would say at last. "Go away, Ina!"

"Well, I only wanted to put you right," Ina would say, and then off she would go in a huff.

If she saw a little girl sewing she would go at once to see what she was doing. Then she would say, "Oh, you are making an apron for your doll, I see. Well, you are doing it wrong. You should sew it like *this!*"

And she would take the sewing from the little girl's hand and make her sew it quite differently. It *was* so tiresome of Ina!

The other children got very tired of her. "Here comes Interfering Ina!" they would say as soon as they saw her coming. "Hallo, Ina. Are you going to poke your nose into our games again? Well, go away."

But do you suppose that cured Ina of her tiresome ways? Not a bit! She simply loved to interfere with everything, and she was so curious

about everybody and what they were doing that she was for ever poking her nose here, there and everywhere!

Now one day she was walking home alone from school. The other children wouldn't walk with her because she had interfered in a fine new game they had made up that morning and had spoilt it for them. So there was Ina, walking home by herself, feeling very cross indeed.

She came to a field and heard somebody laughing. It was such a funny high little laugh that Ina stopped to see who it could be. She climbed on the gate and peeped into the field. And there she saw a most surprising sight.

She saw four little brownie-men playing leapfrog! They were having a fine game, and were shouting and

laughing in little bird-like voices. Ina watched them for a while and then she called to them.

"You know, that's not the right way to play leapfrog! You want to bend down with your back to the others, not with your front. Look, I'll show you!"

She climbed over the gate and jumped down into the field. She ran to the surprised brownies. She took hold of one of them and bent him down. He

stood up again angrily.

"How dare you push me about!" he cried, in a voice like a thrush's, clear and high. "Go away, you interfering little girl!"

"But I'm only trying to show you how to play leapfrog properly!" said Ina crossly. "Bend down!"

She tried to bend the brownie over again, but he pushed her away and slapped her fingers.

"We play leapfrog the brownie way, not *your* way!" he said. "Brothers, who is this bad-mannered child?"

One of the brownies looked closely at Ina. Then he laughed. "I've heard of her!" he said. "It's Interfering Ina! She pokes her silly little nose into everything and makes herself such a nuisance!"

"Oh, she does, does she?" said the first brownie, glaring at Ina. "Well, every time she interferes in future and pokes her nose into other people's business her nose will get longer! Ha ha! That will be funny!"

He jumped high into the air, turned head over heels, and sprang right over the hedge. The others followed, and Ina was left alone in the field, a little frightened and very cross.

She went home. "Silly little fellows!" she said, feeling her pretty little nose. "As if anything they said would come true!"

She had her dinner, and then she went out to play in the garden. She heard the little boy next door talking to his rabbit as he cleaned out its hutch.

Ina stood on a box and looked over the wall. "Jimmy," she said, "you shouldn't clean out a hutch that way. You should have the clean hay ready before you take out the old hay. You should..."

Jimmy stared up at her – and then he stared again. Something funny had happened to Ina's nice little nose. It had grown quite an inch longer.

"What have you done to your nose, Ina?" asked Jimmy in surprise. "It

does look funny!"

Ina felt her nose in alarm. Gracious! It did feel long! She rushed indoors and looked at herself in the glass. Yes – it had grown a whole inch longer, and her face looked funny with such a long nose. Ina was ashamed and frightened.

"I shall have to say I bumped it and it swelled," said the little girl to herself. She did not usually tell stories, but she felt too ashamed to say that it had grown long because she had interfered.

So when she went to school that afternoon and the other children asked her what had happened to her nose she

told them a story. "I bumped it and it swelled," she said.

"Funny sort of swelling," said John. "It isn't really big – it's just *long*."

Ina forgot about her nose after a bit, for there came a handwork lesson, which she loved. The children were making toys. Ina looked at the little boy next to her.

"What are you making?" she said.

"I'm making an engine," he said.

"That's not the way to make an engine!" said Ina scornfully. "Give it to me. Look – you should put the funnel *here!*" She pressed so hard on the funnel that it broke!

"Oh, you interferer!" said the little boy, almost in tears, for he had been very proud of his engine. "Oooooh! What's happening to your nose, Ina?"

What indeed! It had grown quite two inches longer in that moment, and now it looked horrid! Ina was quite ugly.

The children shouted with laughter.

"Ina's nose is getting longer and longer so that she can poke it into other people's business very easily!" said Joan.

Well, before the day was ended Ina's nose was six inches long. Imagine it! It stuck out from her face and made her look very strange indeed. Her mother was simply horrified when she saw it.

"Ina! What have you done with your nose?"

"Nothing," said Ina sulkily. It was no use saying that she had bumped it, because Mummy simply wouldn't believe her.

"But something's happened to it, something horrid!" said her mother, "I must take you to the doctor."

So Ina went to the doctor, and first he laughed when he saw her nose, and then he looked grave, and last of all he looked puzzled.

"I've never seen such a nose," he said. "How did she get it?"

"She won't tell me," said Ina's mother. Then Ina began to cry and she told all that had happened – how she had interfered with the brownies and they had said her nose would grow bigger every time she stuck it into somebody else's business!

"Dear me!" said the doctor in surprise. "So that's what happened. Well, I'm afraid I can't do anything about it."

"But can't you tell us how to cure her nose?" asked Ina's mother,

beginning to cry too. "She was such a pretty girl, and now she is so ugly."

"Well, I can only say that perhaps if she stops interfering with other people her nose may go back to its right size," said the doctor. "But that rests with Ina herself, poor child!"

They went home, the mother very sad and upset. So was poor Ina.

"Now listen, Ina," said her mother. "We can't have your nose growing any longer, can we? Well, you must stop poking it into things that don't concern you. You mustn't interfere any more. You had better ask the other children to help you."

79

"All right, Mummy, I will," said Ina. And she went out to find her friends. She told them what the doctor had said.

"So please will you all help me?" she begged. "If I come and interfere, stop me at once, because if you don't my nose will grow down to my toes, and maybe I'll have to tie a knot in it to stop myself from tripping over it!"

"We'll all help you, Ina," said the children kindly. Children are always kind when they see someone in trouble, and these children couldn't bear to see Ina crying tears all down her long nose. They had often been cross with her, but now they only wanted to help her.

So the next few days you should have seen what happened. Every time Ina came to interfere or to poke her nose into something that was nothing to do with her they spoke at once. "Ina! Remember! Don't interfere!"

Then Ina would go red and say, "Sorry! I nearly forgot!"

In a week's time her nose was almost the right size again, and soon it will be the same pretty little nose she had before.

But goodness knows how long the magic will last! She will have to be careful all her life not to interfere just in *case* her nose shoots out again! Poor Ina! She still looks a bit funny, but I hope that next time I see her she will look her old pretty little self.

A Spell
for a Lazy Boy

Tom was one of those boys who are always late for breakfast, late for school, last out at playtime, and behind in all their work. He was lazy and slow, and he just wouldn't be quick.

Now one day his father called to him and spoke kindly but sternly to him. "Listen, Tom. I am going to give you a reward if you try to alter yourself. You will be one of the useless people in the world when you grow up if you don't stir yourself up a bit, and really try not to be late or slow in everything. If for a whole week you are in time for everything, and even first at some things, and make a few runs in cricket, then I will give you a new bicycle."

"Oooh!" said Tom, his eyes opening

wide. All his friends had bicycles, but his father had never given him one because Tom never seemed to try hard at anything, and really didn't deserve one.

"Now, are you going to try hard?" said his father. Tom nodded, and his eyes shone. A new bicycle! One with a loud bell and a pump. Goodness, how fast he would go and what fun he would have with the other boys!

But although he had such a lovely reward offered to him, Tom didn't feel at all sure that he would be able to be first in anything, or even quick. He sat and thought about it.

"If I could get a spell to help me it would make things much easier," he

said to himself. "I'll go to the old woman who lives in the heart of the wood. People say that her grandmother was a witch, so maybe she knows a few spells."

Well, the old woman did. She gave Tom a little yellow pill in a box. "That's the finest spell I know for laziness," she said. "It gets into your arms and legs almost at once and makes them quick and strong and active. You'll be all right if you take that. But mind – if you get that bicycle because of my spell, I shall expect you to ride my errands on it twice a week!"

"Oh, I will, I will!" promised Tom, and ran off with the little yellow pill. He took it before he went to bed that night.

He fell asleep at once. The spell worked away inside him all the night. It got into his arms and legs, and into his fingers and toes. It awoke him in the morning.

Tom began to yawn and stretch himself as he always did. But his legs

gave him no time to do that – they leapt out of bed at once! Tom got a great surprise. But he soon had an even greater one. His arms began to work at top speed, and he found himself putting on pants and shirt and sweater and jeans faster than he had ever done before!

"Goodness!" said Tom, trying to stop his hands from putting on two shoes at once. But the spell was too strong – he couldn't stop himself at all. On went his shoes, and the laces were tied up in a twinkling.

Then his legs took charge of him again and raced him down the stairs at

top speed. He fell over the cat and bumped his head. He made such a noise that his father was cross.

"Tom! Is there any need to upset the whole household like this? What are you doing?"

Tom's legs had rushed him to the breakfast table, and now his hands were helping him to his breakfast, shaking cereal out of a packet, emptying milk and sugar on to his plate, and then making him eat so quickly that he almost choked.

Up and down to his mouth went the spoon, and poor Tom had no time to swallow one mouthful before the next was at his lips.

"Tom! Don't gobble like that!" said his mother. "Why are you in such a hurry? Yesterday you were so lazy that you took hours over your meal, and today you gobble so fast that you choke. Behave yourself!"

It was the same with his boiled egg. His hand hacked off the top, and then the spoon dived in and out, and his other hand took bread and butter to his mouth at top speed, so that the egg and bread were finished in about half a minute.

"Tom!" said his father, laying down his paper. "Tom! If you think that this strange behaviour will make me give you a bicycle you are quite mistaken. You are being very silly. Sit back and be quiet whilst we finish our meal. I am ashamed of you."

But Tom could not sit back and be quiet whilst that spell was in him. His legs jumped up and ran him to his school satchel. His hands piled all his books in. They snatched his cap and jacket, and put them on. Then his legs rushed him to his father and mother to say goodbye, and then he tore out of the house and down the road. He felt rather sick. It wasn't at all good for him to gobble his breakfast like that.

"What's come over Tom?" said his mother in alarm. "You shouldn't have promised him a bicycle, Daddy, if it makes him behave like this!"·

School was dreadful for poor Tom that morning. He was the first there, of course. The others didn't come for half an hour. But Tom's legs were not going to be lazy, and neither were his hands. They were soon hard at work, pulling up weeds in the school garden, piling them into a barrow, and running the barrow at top speed to the rubbish heap.

The headmaster was most amazed when he arrived and saw what was

happening. Could this be Lazy Tom? Could this be the slowest child in the school, weeding at top speed and wheeling the heavy barrow to the rubbish heap so quickly?

It was too good to be true.

Tom felt very tired when school began. He wasn't used to such hurrying and such hard work. He sank down into his seat thankfully. At any rate, he would get a rest now.

But, no, he didn't. His hands set to work at his sums and copied them down at such a speed that Tom could hardly see the figures. Then the spell began to work inside his head and his brain made him do the sums. He

89

couldn't think of anything else but sums. Usually he looked out of the window or round at the other children, lazing away his time. He couldn't do that this morning.

"You've done enough sums now, Tom," said the master in surprise. "You've done very well. I am pleased with you."

That made Tom glad, but he was feeling very alarmed now. This spell was much too powerful for him. He didn't like doing everything at such a pace. But it was just the same in the writing lessons.

The children were told to copy out a page in their history book in their best writing. At once Tom's fingers got to work and they wrote page after page. The master stared in astonishment. Tom usually wrote about half a page, but there he was turning over page after page, filling it with writing. Whatever could have happened?

When playtime came Tom's legs shot him off to the cloakroom to get his

lunch, and then shot him out to the playground, almost knocking over one or two children.

"What's the hurry now? What's the hurry?" they shouted, and gave him a push. "Stop rushing like this, Tom. It's not funny."

The children played games in the playground, and Tom ran about fast and dodged here and there, caught all the others easily, and knocked quite a lot over. The children didn't understand what was happening, and they were cross. Peter gave Tom a slap, and at once Tom's fists doubled themselves up and began to hit Peter.

"A fight, a fight!" cried the boys, and came round. Tom didn't want to fight. He liked Peter. But his fists wouldn't stop lashing out at him. Then the master came up and spoke sternly and sent Tom indoors.

Tom sat down, breathless. He was tired and frightened. He wished he had never asked the old woman for a spell.

School went on for the rest of the morning, and in geography Tom drew six different maps, much to the astonishment of the teacher. He also learnt three pages of poetry, three times as much as any other pupil. He simply couldn't stop himself from working at top speed.

His legs raced him home for dinner, and his hands made him gobble again.

His mother was alarmed.

"Tom!" she said. "What has happened to you? Tell me, dear! It's almost as if you are under a spell!"

"Oh, Mother, I am!" said poor Tom. "I asked the old woman in the wood for a spell to make me quick instead of lazy and slow, and she gave me one, because I did so badly want to earn that bicycle. But the spell's too strong. Whatever am I to do?"

"I'll take you to the old woman at once," said his mother. "If she doesn't take away the spell you'll be tired out. Come along."

So they went to the wood. His mother had to run all the way, because Tom's legs didn't seem able to walk. The old woman laughed when she heard what the spell had been doing to him.

"I'm sorry," she said. "It only works like that on a really lazy boy, one who has never in his life tried to be quick or punctual or hard-working. I didn't think Tom was as bad as that."

"Please take the spell away," begged poor Tom. But the old woman couldn't.

"You'll have to put up with it for a day or two," she said, "but if after that you yourself try to be quick and early and work hard, the spell will gradually die away. But if you get lazy again I'm afraid it will come back, and you'll do everything at top speed, and annoy everyone, and get very tired."

So Tom put up with it for two days more, and then the spell seemed to die away. Tom tried hard to be early for everything, and to work hard after that, and he found it wasn't so difficult as it seemed. But, dear me, he had only to get lazy for a few minutes to start up that top-speed spell once more. You will be glad to know he got his bicycle!

Are you a lazy child? Tell your mother to let me know, and I'll see if I can get a top-speed spell for you and cure you, too!

The Surprising Broom

Benny and Anna had both been naughty. They had been rude and disobedient, and their mother was very cross with them.

"You are not at all nice children lately," she said. "You don't try to help me in any way. I am very angry with you. You want a good punishment!"

Now their mother hardly ever punished them, so Benny and Anna didn't feel at all upset. They didn't even say they were sorry.

"I've got to go out and do some shopping," said Mother. "You two can really do some hard work for me for a change. You can take the big broom and sweep out the yard. It is full of bits and pieces, and I haven't time to do it."

"Oh, Mother! We do hate sweeping," said Benny sulkily. But Mother for once took no notice. She picked up her basket and went out to do her shopping.

The two children looked at one another sulkily. "You have the first sweep," said Anna.

"That's just like a girl!" said Benny. "No – you're the bigger of us two. You begin first."

"Benny! Don't be mean!" cried Anna, and she smacked her brother hard. Then, of course, there was a quarrel, and in the middle of it a funny old lady came by and watched from over the yard fence.

"What's the matter?" she called.

The children stopped fighting for a moment and looked at the old woman.

"Our mother says we are to sweep the yard and we don't want to," said Benny. "It's hard work. I think Anna ought to begin as she's the bigger one – and she says I ought to because I am a boy!"

"Dear, dear!" said the old lady. "Is it such hard work to sweep a little yard like this? Well, well – if you like to give me some coins out of your money-box, I will sell you a spell that will make the broom sweep the whole yard by itself."

Well, you can guess that Benny and Anna were surprised to hear that! A spell! What fun! They ran to get their money-boxes at once. Benny had ten pence in his and Anna had twenty pence in hers. Thirty pence altogether.

They gave the money to the old woman. She picked up the broom and rubbed some yellow stuff on it,

muttering some strange-sounding words as she did so. Then she smiled a funny smile, nodded her head, and went off down the road, her green eyes twinkling brightly.

The broom leaned against the fence. It grew a little head at the top and winked at Benny.

"Look at that, Anna!" said Benny excitedly. "Hey, Broom – do your work. Sweep, sweep, sweep!"

The broom stood itself up. The little head nodded and grinned. It really was a very wicked-looking head! And then the broom began to sweep.

My word, how it swept that yard! It was marvellous! It swept it far, far better than the children would have done. Anna and Benny were delighted.

"That's right! Sweep up all the rubbish!" shouted Benny, dancing about for joy. It was such fun to see a broom sweeping all by itself with nobody holding it at all.

The broom began to whistle as it swept. The little head pursed its

funny lips and a cheery, magic-sounding tune came from them in a whistle as clear as a blackbird's.

"Sweeeeeeep, sweeeeep, sweeeeep!" went the broom all over the yard. Dust was swept up, paper was cleared into a heap, bits and pieces went into a neat pile. The job was soon done, I can tell you!

"Thank you so much, Broom," said Anna, pleased. "Now you can have a rest. You've done well."

The broom looked at Anna and then at Benny, and went on whistling its funny little tune. It didn't seem to want a rest. It swished itself over towards Anna's doll's pram, and swept it right over on to its side. The dolls fell out, and all the blankets and rugs

fell out too. The broom swept the whole lot over to the pile of dust.

Anna gave a scream. "Oh! You wicked broom! You've knocked my pram over! Stop sweeping away my poor dolls!"

But the dolls were now on the top of the dust-pile! Then the broom scurried over to where Benny had put his toy fort and soldiers. Crash! Over went the fort, and down went all the soldiers – and off they were swept to the dust heap.

It was Benny's turn to be angry then – but the broom didn't seem to care at all. It just went on whistling and sweeping, its little head nodding and smiling all the time.

It went to the dustbin. It swept hard

against it, and over it went. The lid went rolling across the yard with a clatter. Everything fell out of the dustbin at once!

Then the broom had a wonderful time! It swept everything up – ashes, tins, broken bottles, bits of cabbage, old tea-leaves – and what a fine pile it made! Then it swept up the dustbin too, rushed across to the lid and swept that up as well.

After that the broom went quite mad. It hopped to the kitchen door and swept up the mat there. It went inside the kitchen and swept all the saucepans and kettles off the stove. They made a tremendous clatter as they rolled across the yard to the dust-heap, with the broom sweeping madly behind them, whistling its silly little song all the time!

Then it swept the chairs out of the kitchen too, and the cat's basket as well – with the cat inside! Puss was so terrified that she didn't jump out until the basket was falling down the step. The broom tried its best to sweep her up, but the cat fled away over the fence.

"Oh, stop, stop, you wicked broom!" yelled Benny. But it was no good – the broom didn't stop. It just went on and on sweeping things out of the kitchen. When it tried to sweep all the things off the dresser, Anna was frightened.

Whatever would Mother say if she came home to find half her cups and saucers and plates broken?

"Benny! You must stop the broom!" cried the little girl in dismay.

Benny rushed over to the broom. Anna followed. Benny tried to catch hold of the handle, but the broom dodged cleverly. Benny tried again. The broom swung itself round and rapped Benny hard on the knuckles.

"Oooh!" yelled Benny. "You horrid thing! Wait until I catch you!"

But that's just what Benny couldn't do! The broom wasn't going to be caught just as it was having such a marvellous time. No, no! It was too much to ask.

So it dodged and twisted and got in some more little raps on Benny's hands and legs. Benny was so angry that he rushed round and round and round after the broom and got so giddy that he couldn't see where he was going.

He bumped right into Anna and they

both fell over, bump! The broom gave them each a good whack – and then, my goodness me, it began to sweep them up!

Over and over went the two children, rolling towards the dust-heap. The broom was so strong that they couldn't even get up! They yelled and howled but the broom took no notice. It wanted to sweep, and sweep it did!

Just as Benny and Anna rolled to the dust-heap their mother came in at the gate. At once the broom became still and quiet, and leaned itself against the fence. Its funny little head disappeared. It was a broom as good as gold.

"Benny! Anna! What in the world do you think you are doing?" cried their mother. "Get up at once. And goodness me – why have you taken all the mats and chairs and saucepans out here? Did you mean to throw them away? You bad, naughty children, what a mess the yard is in!"

Benny and Anna picked themselves up, dusty and dirty, their faces tear-stained and their hair untidy. They were both crying.

"Mother! It wasn't our fault. It was that horrid broom!" wept Anna. "It's grown a little head – and it began to sweep everything up, even us! We couldn't stop it."

Mother looked round at the broom. It had no head now. It was a good, quiet, well-behaved broom, leaning against the fence. Mother was very angry.

"I don't know how you expect me to believe fairy-tales about my broom growing a head and sweeping things out of my kitchen! It's never behaved like that with *me!* You are disgraceful children. Go straight indoors and up to bed!"

Mother went indoors with her shopping bag. The children followed her, crying. Just as they were going into the kitchen, a voice called them. They turned, and saw the old woman who had rubbed the spell on the broom.

"That broom will always be ready to sweep you up if you don't behave yourselves!" she called. "Just you be careful now!"

So they are being very careful – and all I hope is that I'm there if they begin to be bad again, because I *would* love to see that broom going mad, and sweeping up Anna and Benny, wouldn't you?

Wanted – A Chatterbox

Once the little Prince of Heyho fell very ill, and lay in bed for many weeks. As he grew better he was allowed to sit up for a few minutes each day – but oh how bored he was because he was not allowed to do anything at all!

"I mustn't read! I mustn't play with my soldiers! I mustn't do my jigsaws! It's always: I mustn't! I mustn't! I mustn't!" he said crossly. "I'm so bored. I'm so fed-up."

"You could have your musical-box," said his nurse. "You like that, don't you?"

"Yes," said the little prince, and his nurse fetched it for him. She set it going by winding the key at the bottom of the box. She put it on the bed, and it

began to tinkle out its pretty tunes.

"Now, you are not to wind it up when it runs down," said his nurse. "I will do that for you."

The little prince lay and listened to the music. He liked it. But very soon the musical-box needed winding again. He called for his nurse, but she wasn't there. Bother! Now he would have to lie with nothing to do, nothing to listen to again! He kicked out crossly – and the box fell off the bed with a crash. Oh dear! Was it broken?

When his nurse came back again she picked up the box. "Did it fall off?" she said. "Oh, I do hope it isn't broken!"

But it was. It was very sad, and the prince cried about it. It was the nicest

108

musical-box in the kingdom.

"Never mind," said his nurse. "I'll see if I can get you another."

So she did – but the tunes were silly and the little prince quickly got bored with them. He kicked the box off the bed – and that was broken, too.

"You're naughty," said his nurse. "I shan't get you another one."

That afternoon, when the prince was supposed to be fast asleep, he heard tapping at his window. Then a small, long-eared head peeped in. It was Big-Eyes, the pixie who used to play with the prince when he was well.

"Can't stop a minute!" he said in a whisper. "Just came to see how you are, little prince."

"Bored," said the prince, and tears ran down his cheeks. "I've had two musical-boxes and they're both broken. Anyway, they only play music. I'd like a box that could say things to me – go on and on like a musical-box, but could *tell* me things instead of playing music."

"Well – I've heard of chatterboxes," said Big-Eyes. "Have you? Shall I see if I can get you a chatterbox? It should be full of chatter and talk – you wouldn't be bored if you had a chatterbox, would you?"

"Oh, that does sound a good idea," said the little prince, cheering up. "Get me a chatterbox, Big-Eyes, do. A nice big one, full of chatter, and talk."

Big-Eyes slid down from the window, almost tumbling out of the big pear-tree he was in. He jumped to the ground and stood there, thinking hard, his ears sticking straight up. Where could he get a chatterbox? A box that would talk and talk and talk!

"I've never heard of one in Heyho Land," he thought. "But there may be one in the land of boys and girls. They have all sorts of wonderful things there. I might be able to buy a chatterbox there."

So off he went to our land, and began to poke about in the shops. He wore a big hat to cover up his pixie

ears, and most people thought he was a rather funny-looking little boy.

"What do you want?" asked the shopman at a big toy shop. "Those are all musical-boxes there. Do stop winding them up. I'm tired of the noise. Do you want to buy one?"

"Well – I don't want a *musical*-box," said Big-Eyes. "I'm really looking for a chatterbox."

The man laughed. "A chatterbox! What a funny little fellow you are, to be sure! Chatterboxes aren't sold in shops, you know."

"Where can I get one, then?" asked Big-Eyes.

The man laughed again. "Well, my boy," he said, "if you want to hear one you go to that house up the hill there – the one with the red curtains. You'll find a little girl there called Polly. She's a chatterbox all right. Never stops talking day or night!"

"Thank you," said Big-Eyes, surprised to hear that a *little girl* could be a chatterbox. "I'll go and listen to her. She may be just what I want."

So off he went to the house with red curtains. He squeezed in at an open window and stood listening in a little room. From somewhere not far away there came a pretty little voice.

"And, Mummy, it was such a nice little cat I couldn't help stroking it,

112

and it said 'Miaow, miaow,' just like that and I'm sure it liked me, so I went to the milkman and I asked him for a saucer of milk, and do you know he gave me one, but when I got back to where I'd left the cat it was gone so I had to give the milk to a dog I met and he was very naughty, he broke the saucer the milkman gave me and —"

"Polly, do stop chattering for a moment!" said another voice. "I'm trying to read."

"Oh, Mummy, what are you reading? I do hope it's something exciting, then you can tell me about it," said Polly's voice. "I won't talk for a minute, then – but oh, I must tell you about something I read yesterday. Do you know, I read in my book that —"

"Be quiet, Polly, darling," said her

mother. "I never in my life knew such a little chatterbox."

"Oh dear – I've got such a lot to say and nobody ever wants to hear it!" sighed Polly. "Well, I'll talk to my dolls instead. Angela, come here. Sit up nicely. That's right. Now, did I ever tell you about a doll I once had whose eyes got shut and wouldn't open and —"

"POLLY! *Will* you stop talking for a minute?" cried her mother. "Chatter, chatter, chatter, all day long – and you even talk in your sleep. Be quiet, you little chatterbox."

Big-Eyes had been listening with great interest. He longed to know what had happened to the doll with shut eyes. He thought that he could listen to Polly all day long. What a *lovely* chatterbox! He hid himself behind a curtain and waited for Polly's mother to leave Polly by herself.

As soon as the mother had gone into the kitchen Big-Eyes slipped into the room, wondering what kind of a girl this chatterbox was. Perhaps she lived in a big box?

No, she didn't. There she was, quite an ordinary little girl, nursing a doll. She looked up in surprise at Big-Eyes.

"Little girl, I want you to come with me," said Big-Eyes. "I'm looking for a chatterbox to take to the little Prince of Heyho. He's ill and bored – he'll love to listen to you."

"But I don't want to come with you!" said Polly in alarm. "I'll call my mother if you make me go!"

Big-Eyes didn't let her call her mother. He muttered a few magic words and Polly put her head down on the table and slept. Big-Eyes touched her with his little magic wand and she shrank as small as a doll!

Big-Eyes looked round for something to carry her away in. He saw a cardboard box in a corner. He lifted the tiny Polly and put her carefully into

the box. He made some little holes in it
so she could breathe. Then he ran out
of the room with the box in his arms.
It wasn't long before he got back to the
palace and climbed up the pear-tree to
the window. He put the box on the bed
and grinned at the little prince.

"I've brought you a chatterbox. The
chatter is inside. It's asleep at present,
but when it wakes up it will talk all
day long."

Well, when Polly woke up she had
quite a lot to say. She tried to get out of
the box. She couldn't, of course, and
she began to talk fast.

"Let me out, it's not fair to keep me
in here, I feel like a caterpillar or
something, shut up in a box, and I
don't like it. I know what a caterpillar
feels like now, and it reminds me of
some I once had. They were silkworms
and I didn't shut them up in a box, I
left off the lid, but some sparrows
came or some thrushes, I don't know
which, and they saw my lovely
silkworms and they gobbled them all

117

chatter...

up and when I came back —"

The little prince listened in delight. "It's a lovely chatterbox," he said. "I do like it. Go on, chatterbox."

"Who are you, I'd like to know, talking to me like that?" said Polly, crossly. "You let me out of this box. It smells of soap or something. I shall smell of soap, too, and I would rather smell of lavender water, I've got some in a little bottle that Granny gave me for my birthday and she gave me a teddy bear too, but he hasn't got a growl any more, it suddenly went, I think somebody must have trodden on him, poor thing . . ."

"It's a perfectly LOVELY chatterbox," said the little prince. "It goes on and on and on – I don't expect it will ever stop, Big-Eyes. I shall never be bored now, never!"

Nurse was very surprised when she came in and heard the voice from the box.

"It's my new chatterbox," explained the prince. "It goes on and on telling me all kinds of things. I love it."

Well, all that day, and half the night too, Polly chattered away. She felt very hungry, but it didn't occur to anyone that chatterboxes needed food, any more than musical-boxes did.

In the morning Polly awoke, stiff and uncomfortable and very, very hungry. She battered at the box and

began to shout loudly, half crying.

"Let me out, let me out! Why have you put me in here like this? Why do you keep me a prisoner? I want to go home, I want my breakfast, I want my mother, let me out!"

"Are you alive, then? Aren't you a *toy*

chatterbox?" cried the little prince. "Are you really somebody?"

"Of course I'm somebody. I'm Polly Jones, and I want to go home!" shouted Polly. "Let me out! Why have you put me here?"

When Big-Eyes arrived he found the little prince looking worried. "My chatterbox isn't a toy," he said. "It's somebody real. We'd better open the box."

"Of course it's somebody real," said Big-Eyes. "It's a girl called Polly. She's a marvellous chatterbox; that's why I caught her, made her small and shut her up in this box to chatter to you. She can't stop. Her tongue is never still. We will keep her here until you are better. I'll put a little bread and milk for her into the box today."

Polly had heard all this. Her heart almost stopped in fright. What! She had been made small – and put into this box – and made prisoner so that she could amuse somebody? Then she wouldn't say another word!

So she shut her lips tightly and was quite silent. "Talk!" cried the little prince, tapping the box. "Chatter away! Tell me things!"

No sound from the box at all. Big-Eyes tapped too. "Chatter, chatter, chatter!" he commanded. No sound came out. Not a word! Big-Eyes opened the box and looked inside.

"Perhaps she's run down," said the prince. "Can she be wound up?"

"No. She hasn't a key," said Big-Eyes. "I do hope she chatters soon."

But Polly didn't. She was afraid to, in case they kept her there. She hoped Big-Eyes would take her home if she didn't say a single word.

And that is just what he did. He carried her back in the box, and opened it, and made her grow to her own size again. She was so glad!

"Oh, thank you!" she cried. "It was dreadful to be put into a box and taken away, just because I was such a chatterbox. I've never been quiet for so long before. You were bad to do all that to me. I shan't chatter so much again."

"Oh – you're talking again now," said Big-Eyes in delight. "I've a good mind to make you small again."

"It wouldn't be any good," said Polly. "I should just close my mouth and not say a word. But if you like to show me the way I'll come with you tomorrow and talk to the little prince, so that he won't be quite so bored. But please, please don't ever put me into a box again!"

So she went to visit the prince and

123

talked to him and played games, so that he wasn't bored any more and soon felt much better.

And Polly didn't talk *quite* so much at home after that! Her mother had only to say, "Oh, Polly, don't be such a *chatterbox*!" and Polly would shut her lips and not say another word. She didn't want to be a box of chatter again – no, she'd soon show her mother that she *could* be quiet if she wanted to.

Are *you* a chatterbox? You are? Well, do look out for Big-Eyes, then. He'd love to know you and take you to the little prince! I expect you'd love it too!

A Peep into
the Magic Mirror

Jennifer woke up with a jump. She sat up in bed.

Goodness gracious! What was all that noise?

She reached over to her brother's bed and woke him, too. "Benjy! Wake up! There's such a noise!"

Benjy sat up in alarm. Bells were ringing, someone was blowing a trumpet, and there was the noise of gongs being banged loudly.

"Oh, Jennifer – how silly of us! It's the people welcoming in the New Year," said Benjy at last. "You know Mummy told us – everyone was going to ring bells and bang gongs at midnight."

"So she did – and I'd quite

forgotten," said Jennifer. "Goodness, I was awfully frightened."

She got out of bed and leaned out of the window with her duvet round her. "There are lights everywhere – people with lamps and lanterns. And there's Mr Brown banging his gong – and I do believe that's Mr Trent blowing a trumpet – how funny in the middle of the night."

Then she jumped in fright because a low voice spoke in her ear. "Excuse me – may I come in for a minute? They think they're welcoming me in, but really I feel rather scared!"

Jennifer drew back, wondering and a little alarmed. Who was sitting in the tree outside her window? She soon knew.

In came someone who looked like a small child, with fair curly hair and a white robe to his knees with a girdle round his waist. Benjy stared at him in surprise.

"Why – you're just like the picture of the little New Year I saw in the papers yesterday," he said.

"I *am* the little New Year," said the child-like creature. "I'm young now – but if you saw me next Christmas you'd think I was as old as Santa Claus. It only takes twelve months for me to grow from a little New Year to a poor bent Old Year. Oh dear – to think of all the things that are going to

127

happen in my twelve months!"

"Do you *know* what's going to happen, then?" asked Jennifer in surprise. "Look – wrap this duvet round you. You'll be cold."

"Oh no – I'm not cold," said the little fellow, and he sat down at the end of the bed. "Well – I don't know *exactly* what's going to happen – but I daresay my magic mirror does."

"Magic mirror! Have you a magic mirror?" cried Benjy. "Let me see it. What will it show me? All the things that will happen next year?"

"Perhaps," said the little New Year. He took a small, round mirror from his clothes and held it up to the children. "This is it. If you look into it, it will show you happenings in your New Year."

"Oh – do let's look," said Jennifer, and she peered into it excitedly. "You look, too, Benjy. We'll look together. Isn't it funny? It shines so brightly, and yet when we look into it it isn't like looking into a mirror – it's like

looking through a window." Jennifer gave a squeal.

"Oh, Benjy – I can see you in the mirror – you're sliding on the ice – oh, you've gone in – the ice is cracked and you've fallen in. Benjy, Benjy, what's happening to you?"

The picture faded away. Benjy looked worried. Another picture came. This time it was of Jennifer – and, oh dear, she was in bed with spots all over her face. She looked very miserable indeed.

"Oh, look – there's you, Jenny – and you're ill in bed with measles or something," said Benjy. "I don't like it."

Another picture came – of Benjy and Jennifer together – and they were being chased by an angry man who looked like a farmer! Oh dear, this was worse and worse.

Other pictures came – of Benjy crying big tears, and holding a letter in his hand to say he hadn't passed the exam he so much wanted. And then there was one of Jenny in party clothes having her hand bandaged – and, oh dear, her lovely dress was scorched and burned, and she was crying bitterly.

"Oh, don't show us any more," she said. "I can't bear it. All the pictures are terrible. Surely all those dreadful things aren't going to happen to us?"

"Well – they *may*," said the little New Year. He had been watching the mirror too. "They needn't, of course. It all depends on yourselves. For

instance, Benjy certainly won't fall in the pond if he obeys his father and doesn't slide on the ice until he's told he can."

"But what about me with measles?" asked Jenny.

"Ah, well – you'll be told not to go and play with a friend of yours who is ill," said the New Year. "If you do, you'll catch measles from her, no doubt about that – and into bed you'll go. And did you see that picture of you both being chased by a farmer? Well, you probably left his gates open or threw stones at his ducks – and that's why he's chasing you. If you're silly or unkind, that's what will happen!"

"I see," said Benjy. "And what about me howling because I didn't pass the exam? Aren't I going to pass it? I do so want to."

"Well, you will if you work hard – but if you don't, that's a picture of yourself being sorry because you've been lazy and haven't passed it," said the New Year.

"And the last picture – of me with my hand hurt, and my clothes all scorched and burnt," said Jennifer, fearfully. "What's happening there?"

"I expect you've played with matches and caught yourself on fire," said the little New Year. "It looks like it. But why do you look so worried? These things haven't happened yet!"

"But they're going to happen, aren't they?" said Jenny, beginning to cry. "They're in the mirror – and it's magic."

"You're only looking at one side of the mirror!" said the little New Year, and he turned his mirror round so that the other side gleamed in front of them, clear and empty. "Those are the horrid things that the year may hold for you. Here are some of the nice ones!"

The children watched as more pictures came – happy pictures of Jenny laughing and dancing at a party, of Benjy riding an elephant at the Zoo, of them both winning prizes at school, of Benjy being clapped on the back because he had passed the exam ... much nicer pictures than the others!

"But – how can *both* these sets of things happen?" asked Jennifer, surprised. "Benjy can't fail the exam and pass it, too!"

"You're rather slow at understanding, aren't you?" said the little fellow, putting his mirror away again. "Any of the things *might*

133

happen, but which happen in the end depends on you and your behaviour now! Don't you *see*? If Benjy's lazy he won't pass the exam – if he works hard, he will. So either of the things may happen. It all depends on him. And if you disobey your mother and play with matches, you'll certainly get burnt. But if you are sensible, you will leave the matches alone – and instead of getting burnt you'll probably go to a party. Didn't you notice that it was a party dress in the picture that was scorched?"

"Yes, I did," said Jennifer. She sat and thought for a long time. "I understand what you mean now, little New Year," she said at last. "You mean that all sorts of things are going to happen – but we make them happen ourselves. Oh, I'm glad I've peeped into your magic mirror. Now I know what to do. But why don't you show everyone your mirror? Let them see the things that might happen, then everyone would be extra careful to do sensible, right things, and try to be good and generous."

"I haven't time," said the little New Year. "Besides – people wouldn't believe me. I'm glad *you* do. I think you'll have a happy New Year now!"

He slipped across to the window, climbed into the tree and slid down it. "Goodbye," he said. "The noise has stopped. I must go and find the First of January!"

Off he went. The children lay down in bed, puzzled and wondering – and in the middle of their wondering they fell fast asleep, and didn't wake until the morning.

Mother came into the room. "Wake up! Happy New Year to you both!" she said.

Jenny sat up. She looked across at Benjy. She remembered the strange visitor they had seen the night before. Or hadn't they? Was it a dream?

She called softly to Benjy. "Benjy! Do you remember the magic mirror?"

"I shall never forget it," said Benjy. "Never. Jenny, let's tell everyone about it. People ought to know that it's themselves that make a year happy or sad."

Yes, they ought to know it, and that's why I'm telling it to you, so that you can make yours a happy one.

And what about Jenny and Benjy? Well, they are sensible children, so I don't think they will fall in an icy pond, get chased by a farmer, burn themselves, or fail exams – but if they do, I'll be sure to tell you.

The Very
Fierce Carpenter

Mr Chip the carpenter had a very exciting workshop. He was always making or mending all kinds of things and the boys loved to go and look at his tools. He had so many – hammers, saws, screwdrivers, chisels – and it was marvellous to watch the way he used them.

But Mr Chip didn't like the boys. "Little pests!" he called them. "Miserable little mischiefs! Rude little monkeys!"

So, of course, although the boys liked Mr Chip's shop, they didn't like *him*. They made up a very silly game just to tease him. The game was to dart into his shop and pick up some shavings and the one who had the most was

137

their leader for the next week.

"It's a very silly game," said Jack's mother, when she heard of it. "And it will only make Mr Chip angry."

"But the shavings aren't worth anything to him, and it's fun to see who can get the most," said Jack. "He shouldn't be so cross and grumpy, Mother. He doesn't even like us to watch him when he's making something – and he's really very clever."

This silly game really made Mr Chip very cross indeed – so cross that one day he bought a dog! It was only a puppy at first, but it would soon grow. "And I'll teach him to fly at any boy who dares to come into my shop!" said Mr Chip, hammering away.

The boys would have liked the puppy – and the puppy would have liked the boys – but Mr Chip taught it to bark and fly at any boy who dared to dart into his shop to pick up a shaving. Soon the puppy could growl and show its teeth.

"One of these days that puppy will be a big dog, and will bite one of you," Jack's mother said. "It's too bad of Mr Chip to make it so fierce – I do wish you boys would stop teasing the carpenter. You make *him* fierce, too, and he's not really a bad fellow at all."

The puppy grew and grew. It adored Mr Chip, and Mr Chip thought it was the best dog in the world. He and the dog were always together, except when Mr Chip sent it for his paper in the afternoon.

"Now, Wags – off you go for my paper," he would say. And Wags would run out of the shop to the paper man at the corner, and bring back a paper in his mouth. The boys thought that was very clever of him. They were afraid of Wags now. He seemed as fierce as his master! It was quite dangerous to dart into the shop and pick up a shaving. Peter nearly got bitten!

"Horrible dog – and horrible master!" said Kevin. "I've a good mind to throw a stone at Wags when he goes to fetch the afternoon paper for Mr Chip."

"No, don't," said Jack. "That would be a hateful thing to do."

The boys found that the only safe time to dart into the shop and snatch up shavings from the floor was when Wags was out fetching the afternoon paper! But Mr Chip was ready for them! He caught Kevin by his collar and shook him until the boy was afraid his teeth would fall out.

He caught Ned and rubbed his nose in a pile of sawdust. He nearly caught Jack, and bellowed so loudly at him that Jack dropped the shavings he had snatched up!

"Little pest! Wait until I get you!" he roared. "I'll set my dog on you!"

Now Jack had a very big wooden engine, painted red. It wasn't big enough for him to get into the cab, which was a pity – but it was quite big enough to take with him when he went shopping for his mother, because it

141

could carry all the things he bought! He used to stuff them into the cab of his big red engine, and take them home like that.

The other boys thought it a wonderful engine. "Be better still if it had trucks," said Kevin. "We could all go shopping together then for our mothers, and use a truck each for our parcels. That would make shopping fun."

"Well, there's only room for *my*

shopping," said Jack, afraid that the boys might want to use his engine for all their parcels, too. It would be very heavy to pull then! "This kind of wooden engine doesn't have trucks!"

The mothers all smiled to see Jack go shopping, pulling his big engine along empty first of all – and then going back with the cab piled high with all kinds of things. It was wonderful what that engine carried! It even managed to bring home half a sack of potatoes once.

One afternoon Jack's mother called him. "Jack! Where are you? Oh, you're there, reading. I'm so sorry, dear, but I quite forgot to ask you to take your blazer to be cleaned when you went shopping this morning. It won't be back in time for the beginning of term if you don't take it today. Will you take it now for me?"

"Right, Mother," said Jack cheerfully. He really was a very good-tempered boy. He got up and went to fetch his engine.

"Oh, don't bother to take your engine just to carry your *blazer*!" said his mother. "Surely you can take it over your arm, Jack!"

"My engine likes a run," said Jack. "It's just like a dog."

He pulled the big engine from its place in the hall cupboard, and stuffed the blazer into the cab. Then he hauled on the rope. "Come on," he said. "We'll hurry there and back, and then I can get on with my book."

But something happened on the way there. Mr Chip had sent his dog Wags out for his afternoon paper at just the same time that Jack was taking his blazer to the cleaner's. Wags had gone

to the man at the corner, dropped the money out of his mouth on to the pavement, and let the paperman stuff a folded paper between his teeth.

He turned to go back to Mr Chip, when a much bigger dog growled at him. Wags growled back. The dog flew at Wags, and Wags leapt sideways into the road.

There was a loud squeal of brakes, and a car swerved suddenly. But it didn't stop soon enough. It hit poor Wags on the back legs, and the dog crumpled up on the road with a howl. The paper fell from his mouth.

Jack was just nearby with his big engine, and he saw it all happen. The big dog ran off at once. The driver got

out of his car, and two or three children ran up. Wags tried to get up but he couldn't. His back legs were hurt.

"Who does this dog belong to? Does anyone know?" asked the driver.

"Yes. It belongs to Mr Chip, the carpenter," said Jack, coming up with his engine. "Oh, poor Wags! He's hurt! He can't get up."

"I'll go along in the car and tell Mr Chip to come and fetch his dog," said

146

the driver, and he got into the car again. He drove off. But alas, he didn't go to Mr Chip's. He drove straight past, and went on his way.

Jack waited and waited for Mr Chip to come, but he didn't. Wags dragged himself painfully to the pavement, picking up his master's paper in his mouth. Jack was very, very sorry for him.

"Wags! *I'll* take you to Mr Chip," said the boy at last. "The driver can't have told him. But how can I take you?"

Wags whined mournfully. Then Jack had a wonderful idea. He could pick Wags up gently, and put him on his blazer in the cab of the engine! Then he would pull the dog all the way to Mr Chip's shop.

"You won't be shaken too much because you'll be on my blazer," he told Wags. "I'm going to pick you up. I'll try not to hurt you. Don't bite me, will you, because I'm only trying to help you."

Luckily Wags wouldn't let go of the paper he held in his mouth, so although he growled a little with pain when Jack gently lifted him, he couldn't snap or bite.

Jack laid him on the blazer.

"Now you'll be all right," he said. "Soon be home, Wags!"

He dragged the engine slowly down the road, trying not to shake the hurt dog. Children followed him, and Wags growled again because he had been taught not to like boys and girls.

Soon Jack was at Mr Chip's shop. He left the engine outside and went in. Mr Chip was sawing and didn't see Jack at first. But when he caught sight of the boy out of the corner of his eye he pounced round on him at once.

148

"Ah! Got you this time!" he shouted.

"Mr Chip! Don't shake me! MR CHIP! WAGS HAS BEEN HURT!" yelled Jack.

Mr Chip stopped shaking him. "What's that? Wags hurt? Where is he?"

"He got knocked down by a car," said Jack. "I was there. He can't walk with his back legs. So I put him in the cab of my big wooden engine, on my old blazer, and brought him along. He's just outside. I couldn't bring the engine up the steps."

149

Quickly Mr Chip was outside. In a second he had Wags in his arms, and the dog dropped the newspaper and licked his master feebly. "I'm going to the vet!" said Mr Chip to Jack. "Keep the shop for me while I'm gone. My poor dog! He's badly hurt!"

Well! There was Jack left in charge of the carpenter's shop! What an extraordinary thing! He looked all round it. He felt the big heavy hammers. He admired the little stool the carpenter was making. He wished he could try out the big plane and the saw. What a lovely shop to have!

His friends came peeping in at him, amazed to see him there alone. He told

150

them what had happened.

"Ooooh! We could take every single shaving off the floor while Mr Chip's gone!" said Kevin at once.

"No. I'm in charge," said Jack. "That would be a silly thing to do. Anyway, he's dreadfully upset about Wags. We couldn't do silly or mean things when he's upset."

"Serve him right!" said Ned. "I'm glad that bad-tempered dog is hurt."

"Oh, no. You'd have been sorry if you'd seen him," said Jack. "Leave those nails alone, Kevin. You're not to take a single one."

"I wasn't going to," said Kevin. "I was just running them through my fingers. They feel nice."

"Here's Mr Chip," said Ned, suddenly, and all the boys ran away at once. Only Jack was left, standing in the shop. Mr Chip came in. He hadn't got Wags with him.

"Where's Wags?" said Jack at once.

"I've left him at the vet's," said Mr Chip. "Got to have something done to his legs, poor fellow."

Jack was shocked to see tears in the carpenter's eyes. He must love Wags very, very much.

"Will he be all right?" asked Jack.

"Perhaps," said Mr Chip. "Don't know yet. I shall miss him badly. Thanks for bringing him back to me in that engine of yours."

Jack went home. He forgot about taking his blazer to the cleaner's, but when he told his mother what had happened she quite understood. People can't think of dirty blazers when dogs are hurt.

Every day Jack went to Mr Chip's shop and asked the same question. "Any news of Wags?"

And Mr Chip would tell him the latest news. "Not so good." Or perhaps, "He's better today." And then, "He may be back next week."

Once Mr Chip asked Jack to bring back his afternoon paper for him. Jack stuck it into the cab of his engine with his other shopping. Mr Chip stared at

the big engine and said what a fine thing it was to bring back shopping in. Jack agreed. He was still rather scared of Mr Chip, but he rather liked talking to him and watching him work. Mr Chip didn't chase him away now.

"Wags is coming home tomorrow!" said Mr Chip at last. He was smiling all over his rather fierce face. "You might come in and see him. He can walk all right but he limps a bit still. Can you come? He's got something for you."

Jack did go the next day, of course. Wags was there, looking rather thin,

and limping quite a lot – but how his tail wagged when he saw Jack. He barked and then licked the boy all over on his knees, hands and face.

"Good to have him back again," said Mr Chip. "Now you come and see what he's got for you, Jack. Just a little present for someone who did him a good turn. A good turn to someone who's always yelled at you, and a good turn to a dog that's been taught to bark at you and chase you off! That's something worth doing."

He took Jack into his little sitting-room behind the shop. Jack stared in astonishment and delight – for there, beautifully made, were three fine trucks, one painted red, one green and one yellow!

"Trucks for that fine engine of yours that pulled my Wags home that day," said Mr Chip. "A present from Wags himself!"

"Oh, Mr *Chip!*" said Jack, and he flung his arms round Wags and hugged him. "Thank you, Wags, thank you. And thank *you*, Mr Chip. You made them for me. They're marvellous. Now all the children in my street can go shopping with me, and my engine can bring all the shopping home in its new trucks. I say! What will the boys say! You won't mind them using the trucks you've made, will you?"

"Not a bit," said Mr Chip, delighted to see Jack's excitement. "Come in any time you like, any of you, and watch me at work."

You should have seen Jack going home with his engine and three colourful trucks behind! All the boys came out to watch – what a wonderful sight! "Present from Wags and Mr Chip," said Jack proudly. "And Mr Chip says we can go in his shop any time we like. What do you think of *that?*"

And now Mr Chip often has his shop full of boys, and he doesn't mind a bit. As for Wags, he's as happy as can be to have so many new friends. He still limps, so you'll know him if you see him, by his limp and his crooked left hind leg. Give him a pat for me if you meet him!

She
Wouldn't Believe It

There was once a very old, very proud doll. Her name was Florrie, and she belonged to Katie. She was proud because she had belonged to Katie's mother when *she* was a little girl – so you can guess that Florrie was very old indeed.

Now the other toys in the nursery wanted to be friends with Florrie – but Florrie thought herself far too grown-up and grand to bother with young toys like the smiling sailor-doll, the blue teddy-bear, the golden-haired doll, and the pretty Snow-White with her black hair.

"If you speak to me you must call me Madam," she told the toys. "And pray don't disturb me at night with your chatter and play. Be as quiet as you can."

The toys giggled. They thought Florrie was very funny. She had a big china head with brown hair, rather tangled. Her dress, which was of blue silk spotted yellow, came to her feet, and she wore brown kid shoes with laces. A pink sash was tied round her waist.

"She's so old-fashioned!" whispered the toys to one another. "She won't play or laugh – she just goes for lonely walks round the nursery by herself. I wonder what she's made of – rubber, do you think?"

Nobody knew. The golden-haired doll was made of rubber and could be bathed. Snow-White had a pink velvet body, very soft and cuddlesome. They couldn't think *what* Florrie was made of.

Well, she was stuffed with sawdust, just as all old dolls were! But she didn't tell anyone this, for she felt a little ashamed of it. She went each night for her long walks round the nursery, and turned up her china nose at any toy she met.

And then one night the teddy-bear saw a curious thing. He noticed that wherever Florrie went she left a thin trail of something behind her. Whatever could it be?

He went to look at it. It seemed like thick yellow dust to him. He did not know what sawdust was, for he had never seen any. Could it be some powder that Florrie used?

He called the other toys and told them about it. They watched Florrie, and saw that it was quite true. She did leave a little trail of dust behind her wherever she went!

Florrie didn't notice it, of course. You can't see much when your nose is in the air. But soon the toys began to notice something else too.

"Florrie's getting thinner!" whispered the teddy-bear to Snow-White. "Isn't it strange?"

Snow-White looked at Florrie. "So she is!" said the doll. "I wonder why."

"I think *I* know!" said the sailor-doll. "That dust we keep finding here and there is what she's stuffed with. She's leaking! She'll soon be gone to nothing!"

"How dreadful!" said the golden-haired doll. "I'm made of rubber, so I can't leak. What will happen to Florrie?"

"She'll just leak until she's empty and then she won't have a body at all," said the bear. "Well, let her, the stuck-up thing!"

But Snow-White was kind-hearted. "We must warn Florrie," she said. So she went up to the big old doll and spoke to her timidly. "Please, Madam," she said, "I've something to say."

"Then say it quickly," said Florrie, in her grandest voice.

"We think you're leaking," said Snow-White. "Don't you think you'd better not walk about any more? You might leak away to nothing."

Florrie was very angry. "Leaking!"

161

she cried. "I don't believe it! It's just a horrid trick of yours to stop me taking my evening walks. Don't let me hear another word!"

Well, Snow White couldn't do anything. She and the other toys watched Florrie walking about, leaving her trail of sawdust everywhere as usual, and they wondered how soon all her sawdust would be gone.

Now the little hole that had come in Florrie's back suddenly got very much bigger – and one evening such a heap of sawdust trickled out that really there was hardly any of poor Florrie left except her head and her clothes and the pink covering that used to hold in the sawdust. So she crumpled up on the carpet, and lay there all alone! The toys were upset, but before they could do anything the door opened and in walked Katie's mother!

Of course she saw Florrie on the floor and she picked her up. She saw the sawdust, and she knew what had happened.

"Oh, poor Florrie!" she said. "You're leaking! I'll have to get you a nice new body. Sawdust is out of fashion now!"

So she took Florrie away, and the toys didn't see her for two weeks. When she came back she was quite different! The toy-man had given her a nice fat velvet body, with baby legs and feet. Her dress didn't fit her any more, so Mother had made her a woollen dress and a bonnet. She looked sweet!

The toys quickly cooked a few buns on the little stove, and held a party to welcome Florrie back. She was so pleased. The toys in the toyshop had laughed at her for being old-fashioned, and had called her "Madam Sawdust". It was lovely to be back in the nursery, where the toys made a fuss of her.

"I'm so glad to see you all," said Florrie. "I'm sorry I was silly and stuck-up before. I'm half new and half old now, so I feel quite different. I'd like to join in your games and be friends."

"You shall, Florrie!" cried everyone; and you should just see them each night, having a lovely time with Florrie. Everybody is pleased that Florrie is so different – except one person.

Katie's mother is quite sad when she sees Florrie. "I wish you were the old Florrie!" she says. "I don't seem to know you now! I loved you best when you were filled with sawdust!"

But Katie likes Florrie better now that she is more cuddlesome, so Florrie is really very happy!

Rain
in Toytown

Once upon a time there was a big toy duck who sat on a shelf in the toyshop, and was never sold.

He had been pushed behind a big box, and no one knew he was there. He was really a fine duck. He was made of celluloid, and if only he had been put into a bath full of water then you would have seen how beautifully he could float! But ever since he had been in the shop he had sat up on the dark shelf and had never moved from there – he did not even know that he could float!

He had no legs, so he could not get up and walk about at nights as the other toys did. All he could do was to poke his big orange beak out from

behind the box, and watch the other toys dancing, shouting and playing together on the floor below.

So you can guess he led a very dull life and was always longing for a little excitement, which never came.

And then one day a doll with a barrow was put up on the shelf near the duck! The wheel of the barrow had broken, so the doll could not be sold. It went by clockwork and when it was wound up it walked along, holding the barrow and pushing it. It was lovely to watch it. But now that the wheel was broken the toy did not work properly, and the doll was no use either.

"Hallo!" said the duck, in great

166

surprise. "I haven't seen anyone up on this shelf for years! How did you get here?"

"I've been put up here out of the way," said the doll sadly. "I expect I shall be here for years, too, getting older and dustier each day!"

"I am dusty too," said the duck. "You would not think that my back was really a bright blue, green and red, would you? Well, it is! But there is so much dust on me that I look grey. I have kept my beak a nice bright orange by rubbing it against the back of this box. Oh, doll, it is so exciting to have someone to talk to!"

"Do you suppose everyone will forget

about me, as they have forgotten about you?" asked the doll, with tears in her blue eyes.

She was a dear little doll, with a pretty face and shining fair hair. Her hands held the handles of the barrow tightly.

"I expect we shall stay here till we fall to pieces," said the duck, with a sigh.

"Well, I don't see why we should!" said the doll, tossing back her hair fiercely. "Surely we can think of a way to escape from this shelf."

"But where should we go if we did?" said the duck. "You would be put back on the shelf, if the shop-keeper found you again, I am sure."

"If only I could mend my wheel, I could wheel my barrow away, and go to Toytown," sighed the doll. "I know the way quite well."

"Let me have a look at the wheel," begged the duck. "Perhaps I can think of a way of mending it!"

The doll pulled the barrow round so

that the duck could see it. Part of the wheel was actually missing. There was no mending it, that was certain!

"I believe I know what you could do!" said the duck in excitement. "Why not take out that wheel and slip in something else instead – a cotton-reel, for instance. That would make a very strong wheel!"

"I didn't think of that!" cried the doll. "Oh, duck, that would be just the thing! Tonight I will see what I can do!" So that night the doll tried to get out the broken wheel. The duck helped her by pecking hard, and at last out came the wheel!

"Good!" cried the duck. "Now climb down to the work-basket on that chair, doll. You are sure to find an empty reel there."

The doll climbed down. The basket belonged to the shopgirl, and in it she had full reels, half-used ones, and two empty ones. The doll chose the bigger one of the two, and climbed back to the shelf with it. The duck helped her fit it into the barrow – and hey presto, she could wheel it along beautifully! The reel went round and round just as well as the wheel had done.

"And now I shall go to Toytown,"

said the doll happily, taking hold of the handles of the barrow.

"Well, goodbye," said the duck sadly. "I am glad you are able to go, but I am sorry to lose you."

"Oh, but you are coming with me!" said the doll laughing.

"How can I do that!" cried the duck. "I have no legs, and cannot walk, and my wings are only painted. They will not fly."

"Ah, but I shall put you into my barrow and wheel you along with me!" said the kind little doll. "You have helped me, duck, and now I will help you. You are not heavy, and though you will not fit very well into my barrow, still, I think I can manage!"

The duck was too excited to answer! The doll picked him up in her arms, for he was very light, though quite big. She put him on her barrow – he would not go right in for he was too big – but she managed to balance him quite well. Then she wheeled him to the end of the shelf.

Just below the shelf stood a big dolls' house. The doll cleverly wheeled the barrow from the shelf to the roof of the house, then down the roof to a balcony that jutted out from a bedroom. Then she called to a big teddy bear, and asked him to help her.

"Will you lift down this duck for me, and my barrow?" she asked. "I can quite well climb down myself."

The big bear was a good-natured fellow, and he lifted down the duck gently, and then the barrow. The cotton-reel fell out, and the bear pushed it in again. The doll quickly climbed down from the balcony, and put the duck in the barrow. They called thank you and goodbye to the teddy bear, and then off they went on the way to Toytown, the doll wheeling the duck in the barrow.

172

They journeyed for two nights and a day, and at last they came to Toytown. At the gates stood a wooden policeman.

"What do you want in Toytown?" he asked. "It is very full just now. Unless you have some work to do, doll and duck, I cannot let you in."

"I'm a gardener doll," said the little doll. "Can't you see my barrow and my overall? I'm a very good gardener, I shall soon find work to do."

"But what about the duck?" asked the policeman. "What work will he do?"

173

"Oh, he'll find something!" said the doll. "Do let me in, please, for I am very tired."

So, grumbling a little, the toy policeman let them go through the gates, and the wheelbarrow rumbled down the neat streets of Toytown. Dolls' houses stood on every side, and toyshops sold their wares. Little farms, with wooden animals and trees were here and there. The doll stopped at the gate of one.

"I think I'll go in and ask the farmer here if he will let me be his gardener," said the doll. "I can see one or two trees that have fallen over. I can see a pond that you could float on!"

So she wheeled her barrow, and the duck as well, through the farm gate and went up to the farmer. He was made of wood, and he had very sharp eyes.

"Oh, so you want to be a gardener here, do you?" he said. "Well, I can do with one. I have too much work to do. Can you feed the chickens and the

ducks too, and look after the pigs as well?"

"Oh, yes," said the doll. "I can do anything. Will you please let the duck in my barrow float on your pond until he too finds some work to do?"

"Very well," said the farmer. "Take him over there."

175

So the duck was taken to a small pond and he floated there in great delight. The pond was very tiny, and the duck almost filled it all. When he floated very hard he made big waves at the edge of the pond and then all the tiny ducks nearby quacked with fright.

The doll set to work. She was a good gardener, and she did her best to see to the chickens, ducks and pigs too. She enjoyed working in the sunshine, but when it began to rain, and her hair and overall got soaked, she did not like it so much.

"My feet get stuck in the mud," she

complained to the duck. "It is horrid!"

The duck liked the rain. For one thing it made his pond bigger, and that gave him more room. He liked to feel the raindrops, too – but he was sorry for the little doll.

"Have you found me any work to do yet?" he asked the doll.

"No," said the doll, with a sigh. "It seems very difficult to get work for someone who cannot walk or fly. I am worried about you, duck. The policeman said yesterday that the little ducklings here complained that you take up all the room on their pond. He said that you will have to leave Toytown next week if you cannot get any work."

"Oh, dear!" said the duck, in dismay. "That means I shall have to go back to that horrid shelf for the rest of my life!"

"I don't want you to do that," said the doll, with tears in her eyes. "I am so fond of you now. And you do look so beautiful since I cleaned you up."

The duck certainly looked splendid now! The doll had rubbed off all the dirt and dust, and his back shone blue, green and red. He was a fine sight to see. But what was the use of that if he had to go back to his dark shelf again! It was too bad.

"If only this rain would stop!" said the doll, squeezing the water out of her overall. "I am always wet and always cold now, A-tishoo! A-tishoo!"

"Oh, don't get a cold!" begged the duck in alarm. "If you have to go to bed, what will become of me? The policeman will turn me out, I am sure."

"A-tishoo!" sneezed the little doll. "Oh dear, I can't stop sneezing. A-tishoo!"

Well, that very night the doll was put to bed in the farmhouse by the

farmer's wife, for she really had a shocking cold. The duck swam sadly by himself on the pond, keeping a look-out in case the policeman came along. And sure enough he did! The duck saw him wading across the field to the pond, looking as black as thunder because he was getting so wet and muddy.

"Haven't you got some work to do yet?" he shouted to the frightened duck. "You great lazy thing! Here you are all day long, floating about doing nothing! You can leave Toytown on Saturday! Do you hear me?"

"Yes," said the duck unhappily. The policeman waded off, wishing that the rain would stop. But it didn't. It went on and on and on, and soon the duck pond was so big that the duck could take a really good swim. The whole field was under water, and all the hens fled to their house at the end of the meadow, whilst the pigs and goats stood huddled together near the farmhouse.

"I suppose the doll is in bed," thought the duck. "Poor thing! She will be sad when she knows I must leave her. I will try and see her before I go on Saturday. Perhaps she will be up by then."

Each day the duck looked out for the doll to come, but she didn't appear. She was still in bed. The rain went on pouring down, and soon people began to say that there would be floods in Toytown. Such a thing had never happened before!

The river overflowed and joined the pond on which the duck swam. Then what a great stretch of water there was for the duck to swim on! The water spread right up to the farmhouse, and the farmer's wife rushed upstairs in fright, for it poured in at her kitchen door!

"We shall have to live in the bedrooms!" she cried. "Oh dear, oh dear! What a dreadful thing! All my kitchen chairs are floating about!"

The duck knew that it was Saturday,

and he thought he would swim up to the farmhouse and look in at the bedroom windows until he found the room where his friend the doll lay. Then he would say goodbye. So up he swam.

The floods were very bad now, and the water was right up to the bedroom windows! The duck swam round the farmhouse, peeping in at each window.

Then he found the doll, sitting up in

bed, looking very miserable and unhappy. The duck pecked on the glass with his beak, and the little doll jumped out of bed at once.

"Oh, duck, I'm so glad you've come!" she said. "We are in a dreadful fix here. The farmer's wife hasn't any tea, or sugar, or bread, and we don't know how to get it, because of the floods. We can't go out, for the water is right over our heads! Do you think you could float off to the butcher's and get some meat for us, and go to the grocer's and get some tea and sugar?"

"Of course!" said the duck in delight. "I'll do anything I can! You know that, doll! I'll go now!"

So off he floated at top speed. He went into Toytown, which was also flooded, though not quite so badly as the houses just outside. He swam to the butcher's, grocer's, baker's and milkman, and asked them for meat, tea, sugar, bread and milk, and loaded everything on to his big broad back! Then back he swam very carefully.

On the way he passed many other flooded houses. There were people at

the windows, looking very miserable. When they saw the duck going by with all the parcels on his back, they began to shout excitedly to one another.

"See! There's a duck with groceries! Hi, duck! Will you get some for me? Ho there, duck! When next you go to the butcher's buy some chops for me! I say, duck, I'll give you ten pence if you'll go and fetch me some nice fresh fish from the fishmonger's."

The duck listened to all the shouts and calls, and a marvellous idea came into his head! He would do all the shopping for the people in the flooded houses! What fun! That would really be hard work, and he would be so pleased to do it. He called out that he would soon be back, and then he floated at top speed to the farmhouse. He tapped on the window, and the doll opened it. She cried out in delight when she saw how well the duck had done the shopping. She lifted in the parcels, and as she took them the duck quacked out to her all the news.

"The houses nearby are all flooded too," he said. "The people want me to go and do their shopping for them. If I go and do it, doll, I shall earn money, and then that policeman can't turn me out!"

"Oh, splendid!" cried the doll. "Tomorrow I will come with you. My cold is nearly better. I will ask the people to give me written shopping lists, and then we will go together and buy everything."

So the next day the doll sat on the duck's back, and he swam with her round to all the flooded houses. Everyone handed her a shopping list,

and the duck and the doll hurried to the shops to get what was wanted. Then, when the duck's back was quite loaded, back they floated to the houses and handed in the goods at the windows. They were paid ten pence each time they went shopping, and soon the little bag that the doll kept the money in, jingled and clinked as she shopped. What a lot of money they were making!

"I shall be quite sorry when the rain stops," said the little doll. She had bought herself a mackintosh and sou'wester, and also a pair of Wellington boots. So she was quite all right. Everyone looked out for the little couple each morning now, and called to them from the top windows.

One day, when the doll and duck were floating past the police station on their way to the shops, a window was flung open, and the toy policeman called to them.

"Hey!" he said. "Come here!"

"Oh dear! Do you suppose he wants to turn me out now?" said the poor duck, trembling so much that the doll was nearly shaken off his back. "I shan't go to him. I shall just pretend I don't see him."

"Oh, we'd better go," said the doll. "It isn't good to be cowardly. Let's be brave and go."

So they floated across to him. To their great surprise he beamed at them, and said: "Well, you certainly have made yourselves useful, you two! Now look, here is my shopping list. Will you do my shopping for me too? I cannot get out of the police station."

So they went to do the policeman's shopping as well, and weren't they pleased to put ten pence into their bag!

In three weeks' time the rain stopped and the floods began to go down. Little by little all the water drained away, and people were able to go in and out of the doors of their houses. The field round the farmhouse dried up and the little pond was itself again. The farmer came to the gate and called to the doll.

"What about coming back to be my gardener again?" he shouted. "The duck can have the use of my pond, if he wishes!"

"Oh dear!" groaned the duck. "What a dull life that will be, after this exciting three weeks!"

"Don't worry, duck," said the doll, hugging him hard round the neck. "I've got such a lovely idea!"

The duck was on the river, and the doll stepped off and ran to the farmer. "I'm sorry I can't come back," she said, "but I've bought a little house by the river, and the duck and I are going to live there, and do all the fetching and carrying for the folk who live on the riverside!"

The duck nearly fell over on the water when he heard this. Live with the doll in a little house – and work for her! Oh, could anything be better?

It was quite true. The doll had spent her ten pences well. She swam off with the duck and took him to a tiny house on the riverside. It had curtains at the windows, and a tiny landing-stage.

189

"There you are!" she said. "That's our house! And all the folk who live nearby have promised that they will call you whenever they want to be taken from one side of the river to the other, duck – and if they want any shopping done, we can go and get their shopping lists, and you can float with me down the river, until we come to the town. Then I shall jump off and do the shopping, and you can wait for me. I'll come back and put the parcels on your back, and off we'll go up the river once more. Isn't that lovely!"

So that's what they do now. And in the evening, when the work is done, the doll carries the duck into her little house, and they sit on chairs opposite one another and drink hot cocoa together.

Ah, they have a fine life together! But they did work hard for it, didn't they?